PARIS, PEE WEE, AND BIG DOG

PARIS, PEE WEE, AND BIG DOG

ROSA GUY

Illustrated by Caroline Binch

A Yearling Book

Published by
Dell Publishing
a division of
The Bantam Doubleday Dell Publishing Group, Inc.
666 Fifth Avenue
New York, New York 10103

The trademark Yearling® is registered in the U.S. Patent and
Trademark Office.

ISBN: 0-440-40072-4

Reprinted by arrangement with Delacorte Press

Printed in the United States of America

August 1988

10 9 8 7 6 5 4 3 2 1

CW

To Didier
who likes to be called
Warner Guy III

PARIS, PEE WEE, AND BIG DOG

Chapter 1

". . . Paris . . . Paris . . ."

He drifted out of sleep then drifted back, settling firmly into the soft darkness.

"Paris . . . ? Paris!" His mother's sharp tone jerked him into awareness. But he kept his eyes closed, his mind searching for the reason for her sharpness. What had he done now? Nothing—that he remembered. "Wake up—this minute. Do you hear me?"

The sunlight, bright despite the drawn blinds, pressed on his eyelids. Paris reached down, searching blindly. He found the sheet and pulled it over his head, turning his back to the voice.

"If I have to call you one more time . . ." The threat only made him put both hands between his thighs and bend his chin to touch his chest. Once again he tried to find peace in the vanishing darkness. "I know you're awake," she scolded. "So open up your eyes and listen."

Moms sure can be unreasonable. Why do I have to open my eyes to listen? At the thought Paris wanted to giggle, wanted to share his joke—with her. Suddenly he wanted to hear her laughter, see her dark brown face wrinkle at the nose, her eyes grow bright as though lit from inside by a light. He wanted more than anything to see her mouth widen into a smile, showing her white teeth. But to look up would mean to forget about sleep. After all—it was Saturday.

"I'm going to work," she said.

On Saturday! Disappointment hit Paris in the pit of his stomach. She had promised not to work on Saturdays. Paris had planned what they'd do this Saturday. They would go shopping—first for groceries, then for his spaceship. He had saved the dollar she had given him for his allowance to buy the ship. He wanted her with him— it might cost more. Then they could buy hamburgers at McDonald's, or Chinese food, or hot dogs, or pizza. Then they could go for a walk, around Broadway—or maybe their old neighborhood. He wanted to talk to her about his birthday party—seriously. In two weeks he'd be twelve years old.

"I'll probably only work half day," she said. "I hope . . . Anyway, I'll call you before I get home to let you know. Then we can plan. We'll go to the movies—maybe. Or, if I'm too tired, we might go to Diane's party."

That would be great. Diane was Joanne's aunt. Joanne would be there. Paris liked Joanne. She liked him too. But he couldn't understand why, the older he got, the more shy he was when she was around.

"I'm sorry," his mother apologized. "I wouldn't have had to work if I hadn't taken that day off this week to go to court. But somebody had to . . ."

Why Moms? Paris wondered. Since they had moved

to their Riverside Drive apartment, his mother had felt
she had to go to court. "It doesn't matter if no one else in
this building goes, I must," she had said. "I'm working
hard to pay this rent, and I want to get what I pay for."
Talk, talk, talk. When Moms started on her Riverside
Drive apartment she never stopped.

"It's a losing battle," she said. "The locks on the
front door are broken, the elevator isn't working right.
. . . I know they let *us* move in so they can charge more
money and give less service. But I'm going to fight them.
It's a better place than the one we left, and I intend to
keep it better."

Paris didn't think it was better. He liked his old
neighborhood. He liked the shouting and loud talking
that his mother didn't. He liked it that folks sat on door-
steps and crowded the pavements and talked to him
when he passed. He liked living near his mother's old
friend, Aunt Maud, and Big Dog, and his best friend, Pee
Wee.

Around his old neighborhood, Paris didn't have to
worry about Marvin. He lived under the protection of
Pee Wee's big brother, Frankie. Frankie was president of
the Dukes, and knew karate. But living here, even though
it was only a few blocks away, whenever he saw Marvin,
Paris was scared. Marvin was fourteen years old, and
tough, and he hated Paris.

"What I want you to do," his mother was saying, "is
to have this apartment clean when I get home. I want the
dishes washed—and did you see how you and Big Dog

left that living room last night?" She paused, waiting for an answer. "And this room . . ."

Paris lay quite still. It was important to keep his eyes closed. Important that she think him asleep, or she'd make him promise. He hated breaking promises. Why did she want all those things done—on Saturday? Air hit his feet and Paris knew she had pulled back his covers. He lay, his hands still in the warmth of his thighs, waiting. A silence spread through the room. Had she gone? He waited, decided to count: one—two—three . . . At twenty, he listened, cracked an eye open—and stared right into a large brown one.

Her nose crinkled, the light went on in her face. "That's better," she said. She loved outsmarting him. He squeezed his eyes shut again, but she warned: "Doesn't matter whether you heard or you're pretending, I still expect that everything I ask to be done is done." Or what? The strap? Punishment? No TV? No going out this evening?

"Just look at this room." She turned from him. Paris, squinting to see where she had gone, looked at the back of her knees as she bent to pick up something. He fought the temptation to stick his little finger into the dimple at the back of her knees. Then she would know he had heard and would expect him to remember—everything.

"My God, Paris, you must do better than this!" She spoke in exasperation as, picking up his newest pair of jeans, she looked from it to the confusion over the floor, the dresser, the chair near the window. "This is disgusting," she said. "Paris, I didn't move from the slums to be pushed back into another slum either by the landlord or by you!"

She meant it. Whenever Moms talked about her apartment, she wasn't fooling around. Paris had his eyes wide open when she walked to the door. "Moms, why do you have to go to work? You promised."

"I know." She stood at his door looking sorry. "But, baby, if we want things decent—somebody's got to work."

He lay listening to her clicking heels up the long hallway to her bedroom at the other end of the apartment. In the old place they had had rooms side by side. In the old place he had never known that one apartment could have so much space. Two bedrooms, a living room, a dining room, a kitchen, and two bathrooms! Paris missed the coziness of the other place. He hadn't cared that there had been cockroaches running crazy with every switch of a light or that the toilets ran over or that the rubbish piled high on the pavement waiting for the garbage men. He hadn't hardly noticed—unless his Moms had started fussing. Fussing, fussing all the time. She sure liked to fuss.

In the other place he had liked to look out the window and call to Pee Wee out of the airshaft. He and Pee Wee used to plan their days in the airshaft. Now his mother wasn't keen on his going out with Pee Wee— unless she was there. "No discipline," she said about Pee Wee. "He leads you astray. I love Pee Wee—but he doesn't have any supervision . . ."

Paris stared at the ceiling of the sunlit room, hearing the heels clicking down the hall again. She looked into his room to say, "See you later. And if you don't want to go to the party, we can do something else."

"Like going shopping?" he asked.

"Like whatever you like," she said.

"And can we have hamburgers—at McDonald's," he sang out.

"Or Chinese food or pizza or something else, yum, yum." She flashed her white smile. "That's a promise," she said. She went out.

Paris heard the front door slam.

"Great," Paris murmured. He loved walking the streets with his Moms, eating hot dogs or pizza. She was so pretty—the prettiest mother on the whole block between Riverside Drive and Broadway, or up and down the entire Drive. Is that your brother? people asked her, because he was so tall. And she winked saying yes. Then they'd go giggling down the avenue, looking into stores and eating ice cream as though they were actually brother and sister. Jeeze, Moms was fun—when she wasn't fussing.

It had been even more fun in the old neighborhood, when Dad had been with them. Thinking of his father, Paris frowned. His dad had gone off because he hadn't wanted to move either. He wasn't going to spend all his energy just to make a landlord rich, he had said. Paris had agreed—at first.

But then Dad hadn't come back to apologize when he made Moms cry. And he hadn't come back to say sorry for not taking Paris fishing. He had promised. He had said they'd fish every Saturday. And they hadn't. Paris had thought he meant in the spring. But that was last spring, and here it was spring again—almost summer, and Dad still hadn't come back. And so he had changed his name from Charles Junior to Paris. After all, breaking promises was worse than lying. And Dad had broken his promise.

Moms had been mad when he changed his name. His dad was a fine man, she had said. Just because they didn't get along was no reason for Charles Junior to give up the good name she had chosen for him. But his father had given him that name. It had been his dream to take his son across the Atlantic to that faraway place. Charles thought Paris a great name. He refused to answer to any other. So Moms and his teacher got together. Now everybody called him Paris. And Paris he would be, until his dad came back to take him—the way he had promised.

But then dads always broke promises. Pee Wee said so. His dad had left home too. Only Pee Wee was lucky. He had been left with big sisters, and a big brother who knew karate.

Paris looked over the clothes scattered around the floor. Beneath the jeans his mother had dropped in disgust lay T-shirts, underwear, socks, reading and coloring books. He scratched through his tight curls then pulled the covers back over his head. Peeping out, he noticed a tiny arm sticking out from the bottom of the heap. Leaning over, he pulled. Out came Spiderman. With his arms and chest on the floor, his legs on the bed, Paris moved the arms and legs of the tiny man. Now where had he last seen Captain Kirk and Mr. Spock of the spaceship *Enterprise?* And his ET man?

Getting out of bed, Paris went to the dresser and searched around. His school books and clean clothes tumbled down to join those on the floor. "Wonder if Big Dog took home my Captain Kirk?" All he found was the mirror—for the first time in days.

Leaning on his elbows, Paris grinned into his brown, round-eyed image. He squeezed his face into an ugly grimace: "Just like old Marvin," he said. The image not being ugly enough, he put his index fingers in his mouth and stretched out his cheeks, crossing his eyes until his image became blurred. "That's what he looks like for real." And knowing he had made the ugliest face ever, Paris bent over, laughing. Then he felt hungry.

He left his room and walked down the long hallway to the kitchen. But the bright light from the living room attracted his attention. He went in. Going to the window, he looked out—over the service drive, over the sloping lawn, separating the service drive from the lower drive with its steady flowing traffic, then over the broad viaduct, which ran unbroken from midtown, to the bridge, beneath which Riverside Park nestled up to the river.

The morning sun, shining against the windows over in New Jersey, glared back, coloring the river gold. Paris looked up at the George Washington Bridge, two miles up, and tried to make out the shapes of cars going back and forth from Manhattan to New Jersey.

He couldn't. But then the droning of the sewage

treatment plant brought his attention back to the view. Moms's view. He loved her view. She had told his dad that if he had to work, he ought to be glad to have an apartment with a view instead of a dump. So—they had their view.

Now in winter they looked at ice floes on the river. In the summer they saw the Circle Line, which went around Manhattan, and the Day Line, which went all the way up to West Point. At night they looked at the George Washington Bridge, all lit up like pretty Christmas trees. In the winter Moms draped a blanket over her shoulders to protect him, and her, from the icy winds, which cut through the windows "right to their bones."

Paris didn't feel the cold as bad as Moms. He liked standing with her, the blanket pulling them together. He loved the feel of her soft body against his back, her round arms holding him as they looked out at the tankers, the freight ships, the tugboats, sailing to and from the ocean. He liked the sound of the traffic on Riverside Drive, and on the highway—as constant as waves beating against the shore. But, of course, there was that droning of the sewage treatment plant. Moms said that "they" had built it there, just because "we" were moving to the drive.

Remembering Skooby-Doo, Paris turned from the window and went to put on the television. He threw himself on the cushions before he remembered food. Then he went to the kitchen and took a container of orange juice. Sitting on the floor in front of the set, he gulped the orange juice as he watched Skooby-Doo being chased by a ghost. Then Skooby-Doo's dog, Scrappy, shaking and scared, accidentally caught a tooth in the ghost's sheet. The ghost ran out from under his sheet. It turned out to be the old landlord who owned the house, haunting it to get the "good guys" out. He had heard a treasure was buried there.

Stretching out, putting his chin in his hands, Paris noticed something shining beneath the television. He reached out his hand and found a marble. He searched again and found another, then another. He and Moms had been baby-sitting with Big Dog for Aunt Maud last night. He and Big Dog had been playing Chinese checkers and had ended up throwing marbles at each other.

Aunt Maud was another who hadn't liked Moms moving from the old neighborhood. "It sure was easier for you and Paris to sit for me over at the other place," Aunt Maud had said. "Why you give up a good apartment to move here and spend all this money?"

Moms had answered, "That old broken-down slum of an apartment? I was never happier to move out."

"Honey," Aunt Maud had answered. "Ain't you noticed? The slum done followed you. It ain't but a block away—right there on Broadway."

"Don't you worry none," Moms had answered. "I just love sitting here with my back to it, and looking out at my view. Don't see why you and Bim don't move. You all making good money."

"Don't you worry," Aunt Maud had said. "We'll be moving. But we gonna get a big country house—with a back yard. Ain't thinking of moving in no old apartment ready to fall in on my head . . ."

"Don't you worry about that," Moms had said. "I keep this old landlord on his toes. But, Maud, how you all going to buy a house? Bim ain't even able to finish paying for that old car."

"You don't have to worry about that," Aunt Maud had said. "Just you wait . . ."

"I ain't worrying none," Moms had answered. "Neither am I holding my breath, honey . . ."

Moms and Aunt Maud loved each other. Always saying they weren't worrying but always worrying about one another.

Paris's searching hand came in contact with something small. He pulled it out. Captain Kirk. He reached under again and, sure enough, Mr. Spock.

Gathering his treasures to his chest, Paris went back to his room. He swept everything from the chair and placed it nearer the window. Then lining Spiderman, Captain Kirk, and Mr. Spock at the back of the chair, he went to stand in the doorway. And taking a marble, he aimed and fired—*zing*. The marble hit Spiderman broadside. He fell over. Next Paris aimed at Captain Kirk. *Zing*. The marble flew over the arm of the chair and fell to the floor. This time Paris took the stance of a baseball pitcher. He lifted a leg and *zing*, threw the marble over the top of the chair, through the slats of the venetian blind, *cr-ack* . . .

Chapter 2

He didn't know whether the window was broken. He hadn't seen it. Paris tightened his lips against his teeth, his round eyes staring at the blind. And how would he know if he didn't open the blinds? Would it make him smarter to know? Would it make him stupid? He was still trying to decide which, when the bell rang.

In a frenzy Paris began to pick up his clothes from the floor. He threw a handful into the cupboard. The bell rang again. Paris stuffed some toys into his toy box. The bell rang again. Paris dropped things back to the floor. If it had been Moms who had forgotten her keys, she would have kept her finger on the bell.

Paris went to the door and opened it. His friend Pee Wee stood there, his skates slung over his shoulder. "Whatcha doing, Paris?" Pee Wee asked.

"Cleaning house."

Pee Wee's narrow, sad, brown face grew sadder. "Doing what!" Moms called Pee Wee scruffy-looking. Pee Wee's face always looked half washed, his hair looked half combed, and his clothes were always worn out where they were supposed to be: at the elbows and knees, and the little toes of his sneakers. He kept his head cocked to the side, his eyes shifting, as though ready to duck. Moms said it was because Pee Wee kept ducking from things before his mother accused him. "Thought we were going skating," Pee Wee said.

"Moms had to work so I got to clean house." Paris knew that was his mother's way of making him stay at home. When she was home, she did the housework—showing him, showing him, always showing him.

"Whatcha got to do?" Pee Wee asked. He followed Paris to the room but stopped in the doorway, looking around. "Wow—that'll take all week, won't it?"

Paris looked around too, seeing the room the way Pee Wee saw it. The clothes he had thrown in the closet had fallen out the open door onto the floor. Toys in his toy box hung half in, half out. A surge of helplessness forced him down onto the bed. For a time the two boys remained silent, just looking. Then Pee Wee said, "I'll help . . ."

"You will?" Paris's face lit up hopefully.

"When we get back," Pee Wee said.

"I can't go out. Moms will be getting back early."

"That's why we better go now," Pee Wee said. "If we do, we'll get back 'fore she does and we'll finish just like this." He snapped his fingers.

"Think so?" Paris asked. He scratched his head through his tight curls, as though trying to scratch up a thought.

"Know so," Pee Wee said. "But if we wait till she

gets back, she'll never let you go. Then I won't be able to help you."

That made sense. But did Pee Wee know how to do housework? Paris kept scratching his head, trying to think. Had he ever seen Pee Wee do anything in his house except to get out of it? He shook his head, no.

His mother didn't want him to go out unless she knew where. And she didn't want him out with Pee Wee unless she was there. Not that it was true Pee Wee led him into trouble. Pee Wee never did anything bad. Yet, he shook his head. "Can't," he said.

"What you got to do now that you can't do when we get back?" Pee Wee asked. He stretched his eyes out curiously to look at Paris.

"Moms will get mad," Paris said.

"She'll get mad anyway," Pee Wee said. "She'll get to fussing if you don't finish. . . ." He looked around the disorder in the room.

Paris fixed his eyes on the closed venetian blind. "And besides," Pee Wee said. "You promised."

"I did?"

"Don't you remember?" Paris shook his head. Breaking a promise was worse than lying.

"You did," Pee Wee nodded his head. "But I know. You scared I'm gonna beat you down Dead Man's Hill," he said.

"Not," Paris protested.

"Bet I do beat you too," Pee Wee said.

"Bet," Paris echoed.

It was already ten o'clock of a bright, cool spring morning when the two boys stepped out of the building. The sky was a clear blue, and Paris, feeling the breeze fan his face, felt a lilt of pride. He looked from the service drive where they were standing, through the flickering green leaves of the trees, saw the river, rippling in the direct rays of the sun, and felt a shock of understanding for his mother.

Paris looked down the Drive at the short, pure-looking blocks. Then he looked up and "the shell" sprang into his vision. The burned-out seven-story building stood only a few short blocks away, its blackened window frames glaring out over the drive, reminding tenants of the blackened eyes of evil.

"An eyesore," his mother said. "That's what happens when tenants let their buildings fall into disrepair. Landlords burn them down to collect insurance." Looking at the burned-out shell of the building, Paris thought of the old landlord in Skooby-Doo.

They walked up the block toward Broadway, and Pee Wee said, "A quarter I win, Paris." Paris felt in his jeans for the folded dollar bill he had saved for his spaceship. He took it out to show to Pee Wee. Then he put it back into his pocket again.

"Okay, quarter it is," he said. But when Pee Wee didn't take out his, he asked, "Where's your money?"

"I'll owe you," Pee Wee said.

"You owe me already," Paris complained. Pee Wee never had money of his own. Already he owed Paris for the last two bets he had lost.

"If I win," Pee Wee said, his eyebrows stretching, making his face sadder, "you pay me a quarter. If I lose, then I clean your house."

"But you promised to do that already," Paris reminded him.

"Said I'd help." Pee Wee cocked his head to look at Paris from the side of his eyes. "If I lose then I do it all. Deal?"

Paris pulled his lips tight up against his teeth thinking about that. He couldn't let Pee Wee clean his whole house. And if Pee Wee won, he'd still say that Paris owed him. But it was Pee Wee who owed—twice over.

Not that there was a chance that Pee Wee could beat him, Paris consoled himself. Pee Wee was thirteen. But

Paris was bigger and stronger. If Pee Wee beat him skating down Dead Man's Hill, it was sure that Paris would overtake him when skating uphill. Still there was a chance . . . "I want my money," Paris said.

"You'll get it. Do I ever not pay you?" Pee Wee asked.

"All the time," Paris answered.

"Not when I got money," Pee Wee said. Paris pulled his lips against his teeth again. He didn't want to hurt his friend by asking when.

The boys turned the corner into Broadway and life sprang up around them. Dogs barked, kids shouted, and women pulled shopping carts to and from supermarkets. And as they pushed into the noise, footsteps ran from behind them. "Gotcha."

The boys jumped and turned. Angelo, from the old neighborhood.

"Angelo!" Paris cried, glad to see him.

"Fooled you that time, didn't I?" The unshaven, toothless old drunk spent every moment teasing kids. He swayed unsteadily over Paris, breathing his sour wine breath into his face. Pee Wee nudged Paris on. But Paris kept smiling. It was sure good to know that Angelo was on the avenue now. Bet Moms would be glad. . . .

Weaving their way through the crowded avenue, they had neared the corner when they heard, "Hey, you guys, wait for me." Turning, they saw Big Dog. The wide grin spreading over his round, full face exposed the empty space where his side teeth were missing. An answering grin spread across Paris's face. He had seen his fat friend the night before. But the sight of Big Dog, his oversized jeans making his big behind broader, his feet pigeon-toed as he waddled toward them, brought a pull of pleasure to Paris. Big Dog was stubborn. He was hard-headed. Sometimes he could be very stingy. But Paris thought him the greatest.

"What does he want?" Pee Wee grumbled, his pointed, sad face turning sulky.

"Where you going?" Paris asked. He, too, had skates slung over his shoulder.

"Skating—with you," Big Dog said, eyeing their skates.

"Not with us, you not," Pee Wee said in an unfriendly voice.

"Why not?" Big Dog asked, his round face turned down, pretending hurt.

"We having a race," Paris said. "Down Dead Man's Hill."

"I can race down Dead Man's Hill too," Big Dog answered. Paris shook his head.

"Too dang'rous."

Big Dog was like the little brother Paris always wanted. Warm and cuddly. He was nine. Moms loved him too. She said Big Dog was the most articulate kid for his age. For both those reasons Paris hated playing with Big Dog outside. Aunt Maud and Moms held him responsible. Paris was older, they said. But worse, Big Dog kept them in trouble. He never let anybody forget that he was a smart kid.

"I'm going," Big Dog said. "This is a free country."

"Ain't going with me," Pee Wee said.

"My skates are as good as yours," Big Dog said.

Big Dog's skates were better. They were attached to boots. The other two boys had the clamp-on kind. Uncle Bim always bought Big Dog the best. He was an only child. *The* Big Dog," Uncle Bim said and took Big Dog with him everywhere, eating and drinking. Enjoying life, Moms said. Uncle Bim never took Aunt Maud out. Said she kept them guilty about their waistlines, while she was just putting food in hers.

"Don't matter about your old skates," Pee Wee said. "You still ain't coming with me."

They were standing in front of Big Gus's store near the corner—the store which sold everything from groceries to hardware. And now as Paris turned from Big Dog, he felt his face burning. He tried to pretend he hadn't seen the tall girl leaving the store. But Big Dog saw her and called out in his high, clear voice, "Paris, why didn't you talk to Joanne?"

Paris blushed. He wanted the pavement to open up and pull him under. He wanted to run and hide from the girl whom he had known all his life. Hearing her name, Joanne stuck her head even higher—the better to look down.

"Joanne," Big Dog said. "We going skating. Want to come along?"

Joanne smiled condescendingly at Big Dog. She looked all the way down at Pee Wee, to his scuffy, worn sneakers, then she brought her eyes to a smile as they

looked at Paris. "How are you, Paris?" she said. But as he kept looking at his sneakers, she walked off.

He liked her. He really liked her. He liked the way she stuck up her head. He even understood why. After all, her family had been the first to move from the old neighborhood to Broadway. But now that he and Moms lived on the Drive—her family actually came to visit them. Joanne had to be the prettiest girl on the avenue, with her thick, light brown hair, the same color as her skin. She had it in one long plait. It hit her back as she walked away.

"Why didn't you say hello?" Big Dog asked, teasing. He knew Paris liked her. "See how funny Paris looks when he sees Joanne? Know why?"

"Why?" Pee Wee asked.

"Scared," Big Dog said, pushing his elbow into Pee Wee's side, trying to forge a friendship, an acceptance.

"There you go you lying-fat-in-the-pants-dog, Big Dog." Paris's face kept getting hotter and hotter.

"You mean Paris is scared of a girl?" Pee Wee said, giving in to Big Dog.

"Scared she'd kiss him," Big Dog said.

"She wouldn't do that," Pee Wee said.

"Didn't you see how she looked at him—down like this," Big Dog imitated Joanne's long look.

"She wasn't looking at him," Pee Wee said. "She was looking at me."

"Oh, then Paris loves a cross-eyed girl," Big Dog chanted. "Paris loves cross-eyed Joanne—who can look at two boys at the same time."

Making a fist, Paris pushed it into Big Dog's fat arm, felt it slide off the tight skin and he ran. He needed time —one second to hear himself think: I like her. I like her.

Big Dog and Pee Wee ran after him. Then they were running and laughing and shouting. "What you punch me for snorty-nose, Paris?" Big Dog cried, when Paris let him catch up. "I didn't do nothing." He made a fist to hit back, as Pee Wee said, "Oh, oh, trouble . . ."

Indeed, trouble was walking toward them in the form of Marvin and his two friends. "Jeeze," Paris groaned to himself. It seemed that everybody and their friends were out on this early too-nice-to-be-anything-but spring day. Even the hateful guys. Paris knew Russell, one of the boys walking with Marvin. He lived in his house in the old neighborhood. The other, Paris had never seen before.

Quiet now, the three boys walked, staring straight ahead, pretending they hadn't seen the big boys. They hoped the big boys hadn't seen them. But fourteen-year-old Marvin never missed seeing smaller and younger kids. He liked to beat them up or take their bikes. He rode the bicycles until he got tired, then wrecked them and threw them in the bushes in the park. He stole little kids' radios, and took their money. He even made kids steal money for him.

Nor did it matter if kids told their mothers and their mothers told the police. Nothing ever happened, except he'd be right outside doing the same things over again. But there was nothing Marvin liked better than to pick on Paris. He hated Paris. Maybe because Paris was younger but almost as tall as he, or maybe because Paris refused to steal for him—and could run faster.

"Hey, you," Marvin said, blocking their way. Paris tried to pretend that he hadn't seen Marvin. He tried to step aside. But Marvin poked Paris in his chest. "Got some talk for you," he said. Paris had no choice but to look at him. "Got any change, man?" Marvin asked.

Paris's first thought was to go for the money in his jeans and just hand it over. But what if Marvin took it and beat him up anyway? That's what he wanted to do.

Marvin was small for his age—not much taller than

Paris—and thin. But he had mean eyes. Crazy eyes, some said. Some said that when they got red, Marvin didn't know what he was doing. "You ain't heard me?" Marvin asked.

"Better leave me alone," Paris said, deciding to brave it out.

"Or what you gonna do, punk?" Marvin poked Paris in the chest again, harder.

"We ain't done nothing to you Marvin," Pee Wee said. "Leave my friend alone."

Marvin looked at Pee Wee. "He ain't no friend. See how he left you. Gone to live on the Drive, ain't he?"

"He is my friend," Pee Wee said. "Don't you be bothering him."

"Look, man, my thing ain't with you," Marvin said. "I only got words for this turkey." Marvin didn't mess with Pee Wee. He was scared of Pee Wee's big brother. Everybody was scared of Frankie.

"You'd better leave us alone," Pee Wee said.

Marvin's eyes slid from Pee Wee to Russell. He didn't want his boys to see him backing down—not from such small kids. But he shrugged, and was about to walk on, when Big Dog, seeing him back down and knowing the reason, said, "Go on, get outa here. Or we'll get Frankie on you."

A chill shot through Paris. Marvin couldn't back down after that. From someone as small as Big Dog? Neither could he beat up Big Dog, whose father was a great big man and lived on his block. He looked back at Paris.

"How much money you say you got?" Marvin asked. Paris fished in his pocket.

"What's it to you?" Big Dog said.

"Look, fat stuff," Marvin said. "When I talk to you, answer."

"I'm talking to you." Big Dog put his hands on his fat hips, shaking his head at Marvin. "And you ain't getting none of Paris's money neither. We ain't scared of you."

Russell laughed. Big Dog did look funny. But Marvin's eyes turned red. Paris handed his folded dollar bill to Marvin. But Marvin didn't see it. He kept looking at Big Dog. "So you want to cut yourself into this action?" he said. "Then come and get these." He snatched the skates from Big Dog's shoulder.

"You can't have my skates, Marvin," Big Dog said.

"Tell me who's got them?" Marvin asked, walking off. It seemed he had forgotten Big Dog's big father. The other boys followed.

Big Dog ran after them. He grabbed the back of Marvin's jacket and held on. "You can't have 'em. You can't have 'em. . . ." Marvin turned back, put his hand over Big Dog's face, and pushed. Big Dog fell backward. Marvin and his friends walked on. Big Dog sat on the pavement where he had fallen. He screamed. Tears rolled down his face. "Give me back my skates. Give me back my skates. . . ."

"Give him back his skates," Paris said, anger replacing fright. He hated anyone hurting Big Dog. It hurt him too. "Give 'em back or I'll—."

"You'll what?" Marvin whirled, glad for the one he really wanted.

Paris swallowed hard, his quick temper evaporating into fear. Still, Big Dog's screams, loud in his ears, forced him to go on. "Or I'll take 'em."

"That's the way you gonna get 'em, punk." Marvin faced Paris, his red eyes narrow. "Come and get 'em."

Paris pulled his lips hard against his teeth. He danced on his feet the way he had seen Muhammad Ali do on TV. But his hands were heavy. His feet, too, felt weighted.

"Why you messing with us, man?" Pee Wee said.

"Keep outa this, Pee Wee," Marvin warned, no longer afraid. No longer caring. "My thing is with this punk. If you wanna join him . . ."

Paris wanted to join Big Dog crying. Only he couldn't. He hated that he had done nothing but walk out of his house and that this fourteen-year-old bad-eyed kid wanted to beat him up, maybe even kill him—and that he probably could. But Paris moved around him. And seeing Paris trying to dance, Marvin laughed. He made one fist, pulled it back . . .

"Let 'em kids alone, man."

From the corners of his eyes Paris saw Frankie walking by. He never stopped, only growled and kept on walking with his friends. But his words had the needed effect. Marvin's hands fell to his side. "You wait," he warned. "Frankie ain't gonna be around all the time."

"He got my skates. He got my skates." Big Dog

screamed. He scrambled to his feet and called after the sixteen-year-old Frankie. "He got my skates."

"Give the kid his skates," Frankie called back over his shoulder. Marvin threw the skates. They landed at Paris's feet with a clatter.

The smaller boys waited for Marvin and his friends to walk away, to disappear, before starting off again. Then Pee Wee said, "Paris, you didn't want to fight Marvin anyway, did you?" As though he had a choice. "That would have spoiled our fun."

"That's right," Big Dog said, wiping his streaky face with his hands. "Paris could have done him in. Couldn't you have, Paris?"

"That's right," Paris said, beaming at the pride in Big Dog's voice and at remembering how boldly he had talked back to the tough. He danced on his feet, with a rise of excitement. He hit out with his fists. His hands stayed high, his feet light. "The next time—man," he said.

"Next time," Big Dog shouted in his high voice. "When you got him looking, I'll get him from the back— *voom.*"

"Yeah," Pee Wee said, shouting to be heard over Big Dog. "Then I'll get him from the side. *Zap.*"

"*Tatatata,* to the nose, to the mouth," Paris shouted, still dancing lightly around. Then remembering he said, "Big Dog, when somebody's talking to me—let me do my own talking back, okay?"

"Okay," Big Dog readily agreed. They walked on in sober silence.

Then Paris said, "Sure hate that Marvin, don't you, Pee Wee?"

"Sure do," Pee Wee said.

"Wish something bad would happen to him," Paris said. "Like the cops arrest him and put him away forever."

"Or maybe he'd bust his head wide open," Big Dog said. "Like when he swings out of the window in the shell."

"That burned-out building? Marvin be swinging out of the window?" Paris asked.

"Sure do," Big Dog said. "Seen him yesterday. Him and some big guys."

"Is he that brave?" Paris asked.

"That ain't brave. That's crazy," Pee Wee said.

"That's stupid," Big Dog said.

"What if he falls?" Pee Wee said.

For a time they walked on in silence. Then Paris said, "Oh, sweat . . ."

Dead Man's Hill—one of the steepest of the steep streets going from Broadway to Riverside Drive—had to be the best. On one side there was the cemetery, and on the other the Spanish American museum, which kept skaters in the summer—and sleigh-riders in winter—away from the curious or overcautious eyes of grown-ups. Paris had discovered it that winter. He had introduced it to Pee Wee, and when it was icy, they had slid down on sleds or flattened cardboard cartons to the bottom of the hill.

Standing at the top now, they could look over the

river to the New Jersey Marina. Dozens of boats were anchored there. Seeing the boats brought Paris to another world. Now that the weather was almost hot, he thought of sailing. Not only up and down the Hudson, but to far-off places—England, France—Paris. His mother fed his dreams the way his father had before. "We'll do it one day," she promised. "We'll take a boat and sail right across the Atlantic."

Of course, Aunt Maud worried: "If you *wants* to get there, honey, you'd better start saving your pennies to go by plane."

And, of course, Moms comforted Aunt Maud by saying, "Don't you worry, Maud. I'll get there in my own way and in my own time."

Now as Paris stood gazing over the sun-sparkled water, Pee Wee said from the curb where he was rushing to buckle his skates, "Let's make it the best three out of five, Paris."

"Can't," Paris said. He sat down too. "Got to get back home."

He thought of his mother standing over him, her mouth opening, shutting, opening, shutting. He shook his head to push her out of it. He had the prettiest mother on the whole block—when she wasn't fussing.

"Two out of three," he said firmly. "And we got to hurry."

"Okay," Pee Wee shrugged, his eyes shifting to look down the street, his head cocked to his shoulder. For a second Paris wondered what his friend was thinking, then he started buckling his skates. But as he was getting up, he realized that Big Dog, sitting beside him, was taking off his sneakers.

"What are you doing?" he asked.

"Taking off my sneaks."

"Why?"

"Why you think? To put on my skates, that's why."

"I told you," Paris spoke in his best grown-up voice. "You can't race with us."

"Who said?"

"I said. You don't skate good enough."

"Do too," Big Dog said, struggling with the knot on his sneaker.

"See," Paris scolded. "That's why I didn't want you to come. You don't listen." He liked the sound of his voice scolding his little friend. It made him feel he was taking care of Big Dog. Big Dog would say he was. And there was nothing that Aunt Maud or Moms could say about it.

"I skate good. Don't you remember?" Big Dog asked.

"That's in the park. Not down Dead Man's Hill."

"I can too," Big Dog said, his mouth pinched together stubbornly. "I can beat both of you." He pulled off his sneaker, throwing it across the pavement.

"Give you a quarter if you referee," Paris said.

"Got five dollars," Big Dog said.

That irritated Paris. That was the trouble with kids with fathers. Always got what they wanted. "Well, if you skate down this hill, I'll never let you go anywhere with me again."

By this time Pee Wee had put on his skates. And taking advantage of Paris's talking to Big Dog, he skated over to the left curb. That was Paris's best starting-off side. That got Paris mad. "If you dare to skate down this hill, I'll tell Aunt Maud," he said.

"And I'll tell on you," Big Dog shot back. That kept Paris quiet. He wondered what to do to keep Big Dog's big mouth shut.

Smug, because he had silenced Paris, Big Dog called to Pee Wee, "Bet I can beat you."

"Bet," Pee Wee said. "Five bucks."

"You can't do that to him!" Even though Big Dog was a big mouth, Paris couldn't let Pee Wee take advantage of him.

"Why not?" Pee Wee's mischievous grin lit the scrubbiness off his sad face. "He might win. Fat boys with wings happens in fairy stories." He and Paris bent over laughing.

"Fairy tales comes from real life," Big Dog said. "My father says . . ."

"His father, his father." Pee Wee looked away in disgust. "Paris, what you bring this simp along for?"

"I didn't," Paris protested. "You did." He skated to the right curb, which was the wrong side for him to start off.

"Ready?" Pee Wee called.

"Ready," Paris said.

"Me too." Big Dog rushed to stand up. But one foot caught in his oversized jeans leg. It pulled the other leg from beneath him. "That didn't hurt," he looked up to say.

"That serves you right," Paris said. "And look, you didn't even lace up your boots."

"Lace them for me," Big Dog pleaded.

"No. And look at your sneakers." Paris pointed to where the sneakers were thrown out in the middle of the pavement. "Somebody's gonna take them for sure."

"Wait for me," Big Dog called as he crawled on hands and knees to the sneakers.

"Ready, Paris," Pee Wee said. "Stop worrying about him. Let the dope break his own head."

Paris lined up with Pee Wee, but his anger—and worry—over Big Dog had broken his concentration, and when Pee Wee called out, "Ready, set, go!" he was late starting off.

Pee Wee darted out taking the lead. For a moment the fear of losing forced Paris to try to catch him. But then he gave himself over to the joy of the hill. He forgot about Big Dog, forgot Pee Wee—even forgot the race. He pushed into the wind and the wind pushed back. It washed over his face, whistled in his ears, bloused his shirt out around him. It caught him in a world outside and inside himself. Paris tasted the water. He felt it tingle his skin, spray the back of his mouth. A lightness of head from the pull of gravity made him a part of all the forces around. He flew down, down, down. The foot of the hill came up to meet him, quickly, too quickly. He curved out

into the Drive with its heavy ongoing traffic. It brought him back to himself. He looked around for Pee Wee.

Pee Wee had already made the curve and had started back uphill. His moment—the moment when strength counted—brought Paris back into the race, and he charged uphill, shortening the distance between himself and Pee Wee. But Pee Wee kept a slight lead, which he maintained, even though Paris pushed hard, harder. As they neared the top, Pee Wee looked back and called, "Three out of five, Paris?"

Instead of answering, Paris only pushed harder. Pee Wee kept the distance. Worse, Pee Wee still had the advantage of the left curb—and with only one more time.

"Okay," Paris called back, giving in. "Three out of five." Lucky too. For as Paris reached the top, Pee Wee went flying down.

This time Paris kept his mind on the race and on Pee

Wee's determined back bent beneath the flow of wind. Paris bent low too. He bowed his head, let the wind ripple over instead of against him. Using skating strength with the pull of gravity, he drew alongside, then ahead of Pee Wee.

Now he kept the sound of Pee Wee's skates in his ears. He moved as he heard them move, kept the sound behind him, blocking Pee Wee when he tried to pass. And then he was reaching the curve.

A screech of brakes drowned the sound of Pee Wee's skates. A gust of hot air fanned Paris on his legs. He felt a tug at the back of his jeans. He heard an angry shout, cursing, a crash of steel hitting steel. But at that moment Pee Wee whizzed by him.

Putting all his strength to it, Paris pushed uphill. He heard Pee Wee's skates fast behind him. He pushed even harder. If he reached the top this time, there was no way —no way, Pee Wee could ever catch up.

Then he looked up to see Big Dog rolling toward him, fat arms flaying air, fat body bending—forward— backward. Paris veered to his right, mounted the curb to miss him. Big Dog breezed down. Once again Pee Wee took the lead.

Paris had to fight now. Uphill. Using strength he didn't know he had, he pushed up. But as he neared the top, Pee Wee went flying by. He hadn't touched the line! Not fair! Not fair! First Big Dog—now that cheat, Pee Wee.

Anger at Big Dog and a sure knowledge that a cheater never wins kept Paris going. He looked down the hill and saw Big Dog sitting in the middle of the street in front of a car. A man stood over him. A crowd had sprung up at the corner like weeds.

Pee Wee was almost down! He was going to win! But as Pee Wee came to the foot of the hill, the man standing over Big Dog opened out his arms. Pee Wee skated right into them.

Paris tried to stop. But he was going too fast. His momentum brought him down past Big Dog, past the angry man and Pee Wee. He curved into the traffic shouting, "I won! I won!"

The man holding Pee Wee was shouting too. He was shouting at the man in a second car that had crashed into his. "I hope you ain't expected me to run over them," he said.

And the man behind shouted out of the car window, "Don't give a damn who you run over. But you don't be stopping in the middle of no traffic without giving a signal."

Pee Wee, trying to pull away, was also shouting. "No, you didn't—you didn't win, Paris. I did! I did!"

"Look, you li'l brat." The man holding Pee Wee shook him. "If you kids wants to get yourself killed, don't be picking me to do it."

"Mister, we ain't done nothing to you," Pee Wee spoke angrily trying to wrestle out of the man's grasp.

"What! You kids retarded or something?"

The second man, big, broad and dark, got out of his car. "You kids ain't seen that park over there?" He nodded beyond the viaduct to the park beneath. His voice rumbled like thunder. Seeing the size of the man, Pee Wee and Paris looked at each other. They decided to cool down.

But Big Dog piped up, "Paris won. Paris won. I seen him. He went around the curve, *zoop*—I seen him."

"I don't believe this," the first man said. "What's with these kids? They from outer space?"

"We'll find out when we knock they heads together," the big man said. "Them space mens ain't supposed to have blood." He came pounding toward them.

"Guess what they needs is a good strap on they behinds," the first man said.

Big Dog tried to get up. His skates went out from under him. He fell back with a thud. "What's with you guys anyway? You all think you own these streets or something?"

Paris and Pee Wee avoided looking at each other. Paris moved away just a little, not to be noticed.

"Boy," the big man said. "D'you see my car? It's wrecked!"

"What's that got to do with us?" Big Dog asked. "We wasn't driving."

"I'll show you what it's got to do." The big man reached down and grabbed Big Dog.

"Man," the first driver shook his head. "To touch these kids is to kill 'em. What we need's a cop."

"Don't need no damn cop to open up these heads," the big man roared.

A woman from the crowd yelled, "Police! That man is 'bout to attack that li'l boy!"

The big man kept hold of Big Dog as he turned to see who had shouted. But a police car pulled up. A cop as big, as broad, and as dark as the big man stepped out.

"Thank the Lord," the first driver said. "We'd get time sure—for messing with these retard—"

Their attention shifted. Paris made his break. He dashed across the Drive, heading uptown. And looking up, he saw Pee Wee skating far ahead.

Chapter 3

They raced up the park side of the Drive, Pee Wee keeping the lead. Never before had Pee Wee skated so fast. They skated until, leaving the unshaded section of the viaduct, they came to a protected area where Pee Wee threw himself down on a bench. Paris, skating up, sprawled out beside him.

Hot and sticky, at least they were safe—hidden by clusters of trees at their backs, and at the front, the narrow walk, fenced off from the steep, thickly vegetated hill which sloped down to the river.

"Them guys got to be crazy," Pee Wee said, his breath short. "You know they was actually gonna beat us up."

"And we didn't do nothing, neither," Paris said, panting. "Just minding our own business." He had been feeling the wind blowing against the back of his knee as he skated. He reached down and felt his naked skin. He looked back. An L-shaped tear made a flap almost to mid-calf. "Jeeze, will you look at this?" He turned to show Pee Wee.

"That guy must have done this with his car!"

The ragged edges of his newest pair of jeans brought a sense of despair to Paris. He tried to stick the torn edges together. They didn't stick. "And *he* gets mad," Paris complained. Then his face brightened. "Think my mom can sue?"

"If it wasn't for that Big Dog," Pee Wee grumbled. "Told you not to bring him."

"Me! It was you!" Paris shouted.

"He's your friend," Pee Wee accused. "I don't even like the bird."

Paris tried to think, silently, who was to blame. Pee Wee oughtn't to blame everything on Big Dog. It wasn't his fault if he couldn't skate good. Then he wondered what the cops might do.

"What you think will happen to him?" he asked.

"With that big mouth . . ." Pee Wee sat, thinking for a while. "He thinks he's so smart."

"He is," Paris said. "Moms thinks so. Says that Big Dog is the most articulate boy for his age."

"What's that mean?" Pee Wee asked.

Paris searched his mind for the exact meaning. "Means he can talk," he said.

"You can say that again," Pee Wee agreed. "Too much. Makes him think he's smart when he ain't."

They fell silent as the sirens of a police car drove by. "Wonder if he's in that car?" Paris said.

"Who?"

"Big Dog."

"Naw, they'd take him the other way," Pee Wee said. "And anyway, 'fore they got to the jail, they'd kick him out of the car."

"Kick him out!"

"Yeah. They'd be so tired of hearing his big mouth."

They stared out before them at the tips of their skates. Paris wondered why everything went wrong when

Big Dog was around. It wasn't that he did anything
bad . . .

"Anyway, Pee Wee," Paris said. "Got to go home
and you got to go with me."

"Who? Me? What for?"

"I won," Paris said.

"Won? You got to be kidding, Paris. You know I
won. You owe me a quarter."

"Big Dog saw you. He said . . ."

"Big Dog's a liar."

"He ain't neither. You're cheating, Pee Wee. You
just don't want to help as you said."

"I'll help you, if you admit that I beat you—and give
me my quarter."

"I made it around the curve. You didn't," Paris
shouted.

"Not my fault. If that turkey hadn't snatched me
. . ."

"Ask Big Dog," Paris said. He heard the sound of
approaching skates and knew it was his little friend.

"I ain't asking that big mouth nothing," Pee Wee
said. "I know when I win."

Big Dog skated up. "Why'd you guys run off?" he
said, pushing in between them on the bench.

"Didn't you see how crazy them guys was acting?"
Pee Wee said. "You wanted them to lock us up?"

"Lock up? What for? What'd we do?" Big Dog said.

"They did to me," Paris said, showing the torn
jeans. Big Dog leaned down and examined the tear a few
seconds, then leaned back.

"They did that . . . ?"

"Sure they did," Paris said.

"Your mother can sue . . ." Big Dog said, his face serious. "D'you know just exactly when it happened?"

Paris tried to remember. Had he heard the screech of the car first? Had he felt the tugging on his jeans first? "Dunno."

Big Dog kept his face serious. "Got to remember, Paris. S'important." He waited for an answer. Then he said, "Well, they sure couldn't have arrested us after that. If they had tried my dad would have . . ."

"Oh your dad, your dad, your dad." Pee Wee waved his hand in disgust. "Your dad ought to keep you home—out of our way."

Big Dog turned away from Paris to stare at Pee Wee. Then he sat back. "Just jealous 'cause you don't have a dad," he said.

Paris stared hard down the hill. Big Dog oughtn't to have said that. Pee Wee's eyes and mouth would have gone down, he would be looking even sadder. He didn't want Pee Wee sad—even if he was trying to cheat him.

Paris wondered about Pee Wee's father. Even Pee Wee had never seen him. Was he as small as Pee Wee? Or was he as big as Frankie? Frankie was the only one in all of Pee Wee's family who was big. But Frankie weight-lifted and did karate. Pee Wee's dad was small, Paris decided.

Kids looked like their fathers, most times. He did. His father was big and he was big for his age. And Big Dog's father was fat—wide. Big Dog was fat—for any age. He couldn't be jealous of Big Dog's father, even though Big Dog's father had a car and took him out. Not when his father was better-looking than even Reggie Jackson.

"Why I got to be jealous of your old man?" Pee Wee said. "My father is rich—richer than yours. He's got a ranch in Texas. He got cows and horses and stuff."

"Ooh, what a lie." Big Dog stood up to look directly at Pee Wee.

"Where is he then if you know so much?" Pee Wee asked.

Big Dog had put his hands on his hips but hearing the question he dropped them. Much as Aunt Maud and Paris's mom talked, they didn't know.

And seeing he had stopped Big Dog for the moment, Pee Wee went on, "In the summer when you guys go off to camp, what you think I do? Hang around this city? You got to be crazy. I go off to my old man's ranch. You should see me ride horses." His face lit up thinking of good times.

"Paris," Big Dog said. "Do you believe this turkey?"

"Sure I do," Paris said. "What you think? Lots of times when you go out with your dad, know what I do? I go sailing with mine. My Dad's got a big yacht."

"Uncle Charles?" Big Dog's high voice went even higher. His moon face squinched in disbelief. "I *know* Uncle Charles, Paris."

"You only know him 'fore he went away," Paris said, with the same logic. He knew that Aunt Maud and Moms wondered about his dad. "You don't know him since he got his yacht. And he takes me all over—to Paris. Why you think they call me Paris?"

Big Dog stared at him, wanting to dispute him. But he didn't *know* exactly.

Big Dog looked first at Paris, then at Pee Wee. He sat down. "Well, my father don't have a ranch—or a boat. But we go fishing on a boat."

"Fishing?" Paris asked. "Where at?"

"At Montauk Point."

"Where's that?"

"Long Island."

"How you get there?"

"Paris, you know we got a car . . ."

Paris sat quietly, determined not to ask more. But in

that instant he heard himself saying, "How come he never takes me?"

"He only takes me," Big Dog said. "But I'll ask him to take you."

"Ask him to take Pee Wee too?" Paris asked.

"You want to go, Pee Wee?" Big Dog turned from Paris to Pee Wee.

Pee Wee shrugged. He had been looking at something in a clump of trees. Instead of answering he went and pulled it out. Handlebars. A bicycle.

"Oh, sweat," he cried. "Look what I found."

The two boys skated over and stood looking at the bicycle. Ordinary, but very damaged. The handlebars had been twisted out of line, the chains were dragging, the tires and the seat missing.

"Oh, sweat," Paris said too. "Luc–ky."

"What you gonna do with that junk?" Big Dog said.

"I can get my brother to fix it," Pee Wee answered. "All it needs is to get the handlebars straight."

"And tires and headlights and a seat and . . ."

Big Dog would have kept on but Paris said, "It's neat." He wished he had been the one who found it.

After his bike had been stolen, his mother had said, "A bike is a once-in-a-lifetime present to a kid. After that, they get old enough to buy their own."

Pee Wee knelt beside the bike smiling, his hands going over the mangled frame. "Never had a bike before," he said.

"I'll give my dollar to buy some paint for it," Paris

offered. "And I'll get more money. I'll sell . . . Big Dog, want to buy my ET man?"

"Got one," Big Dog answered.

Paris waited for Big Dog to offer part of his five dollars. When he didn't, he said, spitefully, "And I'll let you have my next week's allowance so you can buy a new seat."

"Takes more'n a dollar to buy even an old seat," Big Dog said. He kneeled next to Pee Wee to look over the bike. Paris kneeled too. It was a hard trick to get Big Dog to part with his own money.

And as he knelt there trying to think up a way, while examining the bike to see its possibilities, he became aware of someone standing over them. He looked up. A policeman—the same big, broad one they had left at the accident was standing there. A little white boy stood beside him.

"That's it," the little boy said, pointing to the twisted wreck of a bike. "That's my bike."

"How can you tell, son?" the tall, dark, broad policeman asked.

"I know it," the boy insisted. "Besides, I have my name cut into the handle."

"Let's see that bike," the policeman moved forward. Pee Wee and Paris stood up, drawing away as though the bike had become too hot to touch.

"It says Bobby here," the policeman said. "You Bobby?" And at the boy's nod, he looked over to Pee Wee, then to Paris. "What you guys got to say for yourself?" he asked.

"We just found it," Pee Wee said.

"He found it," Big Dog said, pointing to Pee Wee.

"Oh—just walked up and there it was? That it?"

"That's it," Pee Wee answered, ducking his head as though to get beneath the cop's stare.

"Sounds likely," the policeman said.

"We were just skating by and there it was," Paris said.

"It wasn't us," Big Dog broke in.

"It wasn't us, what?" the cop asked.

"Was it us?" Big Dog turned to the little boy. The boy looked from one to the other of them.

"Well?" the policeman asked.

"Wasn't him," the boy pointed to Big Dog.

"Wasn't me, neither," Paris said. He looked at Pee Wee. But Pee Wee wasn't talking. He had moved around so that his skates pointed uptown. And although the tips of his fingers were in the front pockets of his jeans, looking real cool, Paris knew he was ready to go. Paris got ready too.

"What's with you cops?" Big Dog said, still kneeling near the bike. He looked up at the cop, that being-smart look breaking over his face. "Even you can see we got on skates."

"Hey, ain't you that fresh kid from back there?" the cop said, moving close to Big Dog. Then Pee Wee made his break, Paris right behind.

They raced up the Drive, listening for police sirens, looking back, afraid they were being chased. They skated

past the giant hospital complex and past the range of hills with the high-rise apartments perched on top. Then, ducking as though from the whistles of flying bullets, they dived behind a clump of bushes and crouched, listening for the beat of running feet. Even when they knew they were safe, they kept hiding, waiting for their breath to slow down. Then Pee Wee said, "D'you hear that kid? About to say we done it."

"Yeah," Paris answered. "Lying. And we didn't even know him."

"Never seen him," Pee Wee said, his eyebrows going

up into a surprised look. "Wish I'd see him just once—without that ole cop."

"Me too," Paris agreed and they looked hopefully down in the direction from which they had come. But when they started off again, it was in the opposite direction. They waited at the intersection where traffic from highways crisscrossed around grassy diamond-shaped islands. Making their way around the different traffic signals, they found themselves going up a pedestrian ramp that led to the George Washington Bridge.

Pee Wee's face lit up, his nose shone with excitement. "Hey, Paris, we can go all the way to New Jersey."

"New Jersey? I don't want to go to New Jersey," Paris said. "I got to go home." Nevertheless, he kept on skating up the ramp. And at one point stopped to look down the Drive. "Look," he shouted to Pee Wee, "Big Dog."

Big Dog, his sneakers on, skates slung over his shoulder stood at the clump of bushes where they had been hiding. He kept looking around for them. "Hey, Big Dog," Paris called. "Up here."

"Whatcha want to do that for?" Pee Wee said. "Ain't he been enough trouble?"

"Wasn't his fault you found that bike," Paris reminded him.

"It would've been his fault if we got arrested."

They stood looking over the side of the concrete ramp watching Big Dog make his way through the dangerous crossing. After a few moments Pee Wee said, "Bet it was that ole Marvin who stole that kid's bike."

"Yeah," Paris agreed. Marvin had stolen his bike and had wrecked it too. "Gets us in trouble even when he ain't around."

"Yeah," Pee Wee said. "I hate him, don't you, Paris?"

"Hate his guts," Paris said.

"Makes it so that it's dang'rous to even find something," Pee Wee grumbled. "Got the cops after us. And we ain't done nothing."

Big Dog had crossed the danger zones and was out of sight. So they skated up the ramp. "Bet I can beat you to the bridge," Pee Wee said.

"Bet," Paris answered, pushing off. He had gone some distance before he knew that Pee Wee wasn't right behind. He looked back to see Pee Wee hemmed in by people going the other way. He had had to stop.

There were only a few on the ramp. But the ramp was narrow. It wasn't fun. Paris was glad. He didn't want to go to the George Washington Bridge. He didn't want to go to New Jersey. He wanted to go home. But instead of telling Pee Wee when he skated up, Paris said, "Race you back to where we started."

Now it was Pee Wee who started off first. And it was Paris who had to wait for people to move for him to skate. Even Pee Wee had to see there was no fun in skating on that ramp. And when Paris skated up to where Big Dog had caught up with them, he was really glad to hear Big Dog, shouting so that his high voice could be heard over the traffic, "What you guys like about this? It's dang'rous."

"Naw, it ain't dang'rous," Pee Wee said. "Not with these high guards."

"Feels dang'rous to me," Big Dog insisted.

"Is it dang'rous, Paris?" Pee Wee asked.

Paris didn't answer. He hadn't thought it dangerous. But he didn't like the feel. The guards were high but made of concrete, giving the ramp a closed-in feeling. He felt trapped. But what could happen? And then Paris looked over the side.

Cars—an ocean of cars! Cars on all different levels to the side of them and beneath them. Cars coming from upstate into Manhattan, cars leaving Manhattan going upstate. Cars coming from the Bronx, into Manhattan, and cars leaving Manhattan going to the Bronx. Cars coming from New Jersey into Manhattan, and cars going

from Manhattan to New Jersey—and then there were the cars going from the Bronx to New Jersey, and from all those places to upstate—on the George Washington Bridge, on the Bronx Expressway, on the Henry Hudson Parkway. . . .

Paris shivered, afraid to move. He kept telling himself that they were safe. The river was nearby. His house was only a mile or two down the Drive. The Park began just a short distance from where they stood. But he felt himself to be tiny—like a little cockroach or a beetle, a little thing without meaning, crunching beneath the wheels of those noncaring cars, driven by nonpeople, mindless cars flowing, letting out fumes with one mighty, continuous roar. "Beat you to the other side," he heard Pee Wee's voice shout in his ear.

"Don't want to," Paris mumbled. He pulled his lips between his teeth, his wide, round eyes staring.

"What's the matter with you?" Pee Wee asked. Then he looked into his friend's face, curiously. "You scared?" he asked. Pee Wee looked around as though looking for help. But seeing no one who might help them, he teased Paris. "Scared I beat you good, that's what."

That snapped Paris out of his trance. He turned to Pee Wee shouting, "Pee Wee, you know you never can beat me."

"Bet you," Pee Wee said. He started off before turning, so that Paris saw the old man before Pee Wee.

"Look out," he shouted.

Too late. Pee Wee saw the man as he was turning and tried to avoid him. One of his skates went over the other. He tripped and fell. In falling he slapped against the man's chest with his shoulder, pushing the man back against the side of the ramp.

For a moment Pee Wee lay still. The old man stood against the barrier where he had been pushed, holding his chest, his face chalk white. Then Pee Wee sat up. "Sorry," he said, looking up at the old man, his head ducking to the side. But he didn't try to get up.

After a long while, the old man finally whispered, "What are you doing here?"

Seeing that Pee Wee hadn't jumped right up, Paris knew that he was hurt. "You okay, Pee Wee?" he asked, going over to him. Pee Wee nodded.

Then the old man said in a stronger voice, "Get off this ramp!"

"Come on." Paris helped Pee Wee to stand. By this time the man's face had become beet red.

"We need the police," he said, looking around at the onlookers and the people walking by. "Can you imagine! This ramp's for pedestrians! Why are they skating . . ."

"We sorry, we sorry, we sorry," Big Dog said, spreading out his hands beneath the old man's face.

Pee Wee was shaking as Paris led him away. But Paris put as much distance between themselves, the old man, and the onlookers as he dared before letting him sit down. He helped Pee Wee take off his skates, then sat beside him while he took off his own. Only then did he notice that Big Dog hadn't come with them.

"I'm not waiting for Big Dog," Pee Wee said, when he saw Paris looking back. "I'm going home."

But the fear Paris had experienced, looking out at the heavy traffic, had the feel of a nightmare. He had to get Big Dog. He couldn't leave without him. "Wait here," he said to Pee Wee. "I'll go get him." Slinging his skates over his shoulder, he started back. But he had only taken a few steps when he heard a voice behind him.

"You kids . . ." He looked back to see the cop—the same cop—looking down on Pee Wee. "What's with you guys anyway?" he asked. "You all think you got a monopoly on trouble-making?" An angry frown was twisting his face. "You kids are dangerous. What are you doing skating up here and running into folks?"

"We ain't skating," Paris said, opening his eyes to show his innocence. He pointed to the skates so obvious on his shoulder.

"Don't be a wise guy," the cop said. "You were! And you hit some old gent back there." He jerked his head, and Paris heard the old man's thin voice.

"Yes, officer. Take these children off this ramp." He came toward them holding Big Dog by his neck.

The cop, seeing Big Dog, shook his head. "Oh, no—not again."

"They're trying to kill themselves—and everybody else," the old man said.

"I was just told about it, sir," the cop said. "And I'm here to get them off . . ." Then he looked at Pee Wee. "What happened to you, boy?"

A lump the size of a golf ball had jumped out on Pee Wee's forehead, the skin bruised and trying to bleed.

"The boy had a pretty nasty fall," the old man said. "He needs medical attention."

"Will you tell this guy to get his hand off me?" Big Dog said. "I'm going. I told him I was going."

"If you'd just stop talking . . ." The old man pushed Big Dog toward the cop. "They try to kill you by running into you. If they don't succeed, they try to talk you to death."

"Come on," the cop said, jerking his head toward the street. "We got to get you to a hospital."

"Ain't nothing wrong with me," Pee Wee said, trying to pull away.

"We'll let the doctor decide about that," the cop said, and holding onto Pee Wee with one hand and Big Dog with the other, he marched them down to his waiting patrol car. Paris followed.

Chapter 4

They bustled into the hospital emergency room, following the policeman. They felt important with everybody looking at them, wondering what had happened. They grouped importantly around Pee Wee, while the policeman talked to the woman at the desk.

Paris wished it had been his head that was hurt. He wished it even stronger when the doctor came out, looked at Pee Wee, and smiled. He smiled at the rest of them too and that made Paris feel good. The doctor touched and pushed at Pee Wee's head.

Then he asked, "How does that feel?" Pee Wee only shrugged, and the doctor said, "It doesn't seem too serious. We'll have to take some X rays. But he must wait his turn." He moved his hand around the waiting room, filled with people—mostly children. "Our weekend bunch," he said, still smiling.

And so they sat on the bench, looking around at babies crying, little boys with bleeding or bandaged heads, big boys with broken legs, and girls with broken hands or arms, and at nurses running in and out from the waiting room into the emergency area.

"I got to call your mother, kid," the cop said. He stood over Pee Wee, book and pencil in hand. Paris felt relieved that after all it hadn't been his head.

"Why?" Pee Wee asked. "Ain't nothing wrong with me."

"You don't know that," the cop said. "She might have to sign you in."

"I ain't staying," Pee Wee said.

"Maybe. Maybe not. But she's got to give permission if you got to be treated. What's your number?"

"Ain't got no phone," Pee Wee said.

"No phone?" the cop said, not believing.

"It ain't working," Pee Wee said.

"Then I'll just drive around and pick her up," the cop said.

"She don't care nothing about me being here," Pee Wee said, shrugging.

"She don't?" the cop looked down hard at Pee Wee. "Well, we'll see about that."

Pee Wee's eyes shifted from the cop to the floor, and he looked sadder than usual. Paris wriggled in his seat to get closer, to touch him. He didn't want the policeman to go to Pee Wee's house and find his mother out. He wanted her to be there waiting for him. And he wanted her to come to the hospital, even if she came in fussing. He wanted to hold Pee Wee's little hard hands. Only boys didn't hold hands.

"Mama, Mama, Mama," the tot in front of them began to cry. The mother rocked her, kept rocking her. But the more she rocked the louder the baby cried, until she was screaming, "Mamamamamama." Finally, the mother stood up and began walking up and down the room, shaking the baby. Paris reached out then to put his hand over Pee Wee's.

"You gonna be all right, Pee Wee," he said.

Pee Wee looked at Paris, grinning, his eyes liking him. "Sure—I know," he said. And they sat side by side, their shoulders touching, until Pee Wee's name was called.

Big Dog and Paris stared at the door to the emergency room when Pee Wee went in. They strained to hear

him cry. Did Pee Wee ever cry? Paris tried to remember if he had ever seen his friend cry. He looked sad. But that was his natural look. Paris had seen Pee Wee look even sadder. But he had never seen tears.

"That Pee Wee—he's so brave," Paris whispered.

"That's because he got a big brother," Big Dog said.

"No—because he doesn't cry," Paris said.

Big Dog squinched up his round face. He looked up at the ceiling trying to think. "With a face like that, he don't need to," he said.

Big Dog could sometimes be really mean. Paris looked away from him, forcing his eyes to stay on the emergency room door. And he was still looking at that door when Pee Wee came out again, grinning.

They sure had made a neat patch on his head. The lump looked twice the size that it had before. And they had tied it with a neat, white bandage that went around his head.

"Why they got it tied around like that," Big Dog asked. "Your lump's in front."

"So I can keep the patch on—till my ma gets here."

"You got to wait?"

"Sure—they got to see her."

The cop had gone after Pee Wee's mother. And all the time they had been waiting, and wondering, Paris had been anxious. But now that Pee Wee had come out and he was all right, he had to get home.

Somewhere in Paris's mind, he knew that his mother would forgive him everything—if Pee Wee had died. She might have forgiven him if he had stayed in the hospital. But now . . . "I got to go, Pee Wee."

"Me too." Big Dog got up, stretching. "I don't want to stay around this old hospital. It's too boring."

"What? You running out on me, Paris? I'm gonna go home with you—remember?"

Paris shook his head, looking away from Pee Wee. If the cops didn't find his mother home, they might take him down to the Children's Shelter. It had happened before. That might mean they'd go to his house to investigate. They had done that before. But he couldn't say those things to Pee Wee so he just walked out.

Paris wondered about the time. It suddenly seemed that he had been away from home a long, long time.

"Hey Mister," he stopped a man leaving the hospital. "Got the time?"

"Three o'clock," the man said.

Three o'clock! Had his mother come home yet? Maybe if he rushed he might still beat her home. It didn't really matter if he hadn't finished his housework—so long as she saw he was *trying*.

"Gosh, I'm hungry," Big Dog said, as they stepped out of the hospital into the street. As though his saying that made it happen, the smell of hot dogs cooking on the cart at the corner rushed down to them. Paris felt his knees buckle from hunger. He hadn't eaten all day—except to drink some juice.

Big Dog made for the corner, pigeon-toes touching, skates clanging. "Oh, boy, hot dogs," he said.

Paris said, protesting, "Look, got to get home."

They waited in a line. And as they inched up, Paris noticed Big Dog's lack of concern. He had been out as long as they had. "Don't Aunt Maud ever beat you?" he asked.

"Sometimes," Big Dog said, shrugging. "But then I start screaming and she get's scared thinking she's going to hurt—she stops." He grinned his gummy, round-face grin.

"Doesn't it hurt?" Paris asked.

"Naw, don't ever feel it. Too fat," he said and shrugged again.

"What's she going to do about you staying out so long?"

"Nothing. I'll just tell her I was with you."

"I wasn't supposed to be out," Paris said. "And I wasn't supposed to take you out neither."

"Well," Big Dog said, getting thoughtful. "What can she do about it? We're out now."

"She can beat me, that's what. And I ain't fat. It hurts."

"But then she'll only beat you one time," Big Dog said, his hands outspread. "And look at all the fun we had." They had now come up to the cart, and Big Dog said to the woman vendor, "One hot dog, everything on it."

"And one with mustard and sauerkraut," Paris said.

Then, from down the street: "Hey, you guys, buy me one too." Pee Wee came running up.

"What happened?" Paris asked. It was funny how

glad he was to see Pee Wee. As though he hadn't seen him in days. "Your mother come?"

"Naw. I didn't want to wait. I sneaked out."

"What if she comes?" Paris said.

Pee Wee shrugged. "She ain't coming," he said.

"Naw," Paris shook his head and said to the woman, "Another one—everything. Right, Pee Wee?"

"Right."

"That'll be two dollars and a quarter," the woman said as Paris handed her his folded bill.

"Two dollars and what? For just two hot dogs!"

"Three." The woman nodded to Big Dog. He was already eating.

"I'm only paying for two," Paris said.

"That will be one dollar and fifty cents." The skinny lady had her hair pulled tightly back. Her black eyes burned hostile.

"One dollar and fifty cents!" Paris stared at her with round-eyed outrage. "I only have a dollar."

The woman folded her arms and stared back. "You don't know how much hot dogs cost?" she asked.

"Not one dollar and fifty cents." Paris kept shaking his head.

"For two skinny hot dogs!" Pee Wee compared their two hot dogs.

"That's cheating," Paris said.

"They're not supposed to be more than fifty cents. Right, Paris?" Pee Wee asked.

"Right," Paris agreed. "That'll make it a dollar."

"One-dollar-and-fifty-cents," the woman repeated, looking around—they knew—for a cop.

So Big Dog said, "That's why you turkeys need me around."

"We do?" The bandage over Pee Wee's eyes shot up in surprise. "Why?"

"Inflation," Big Dog said, taking out his five-dollar bill. Handing it to the lady, he added graciously, "And some sodas—please."

They walked slowly down toward the drive eating hot dogs and sipping their sodas through straws. Paris felt good again. It was great that Big Dog had proven to Pee Wee how nice he could be. And it was great that he hadn't run off and left Pee Wee. He wouldn't have liked that. Paris remembered how upset he had been leaving the hospital. He tried to remember other reasons. But biting into his hot dog, sipping soda, and walking with his friends, he only knew that he was glad not to have deserted Pee Wee.

On the Drive they crossed over to the parkside and ambled along to the steps that would take them down to the river. Walking through the tunnel beneath the highway into the park, they stopped to watch some big boys playing basketball in the playground. They moved off and stood peering through the mesh wire fence into the handball court where grown-ups played handball. Leaning against the fence, they finished their hot dogs, and still sipping their sodas, strolled along with others enjoying the day.

At the guard rail that bordered the river, they

looked through at an elderly man sitting on a rock beneath a tree, fishing. He wore a floppy, canvas hat over his gray hair, and he had a pipe stuck in the corner of his mouth. As they looked at him, he took out the pipe, spat, and put it back in; then leaning against the tree, he gazed serenely over his line.

The boys moved a distance away. They finished their

sodas, put their bottles into a rubbish bin, threw their skates through the iron rails, and climbed over it. They stood for some time looking at the big rocks that jutted out into the river, gazing in wonder at a tugboat that pushed a barge the size of a little island downstream.

"Man, it's hot," Big Dog said. Taking off his shirt, he threw himself down on the narrow strip of grass bordering the water. "Feels like summer already. Be glad when it's holiday time, won't you, Paris?"

Big Dog's fat, sweaty arms gleamed in the sun. "Big Dog," Paris said. "You gonna catch cold." But his mother-sounding words, and the sun being so far west, brought his guilt surging back. She must be home already. Half day, she said. He stood ready to go. But then he saw a freighter sailing down river. Sailors were on deck and Paris waved. They waved back. Pee Wee and Big Dog got up and started waving too.

"Know where they going? To the Atlantic Ocean. Maybe even to Paris." Paris said, thinking of his father.

"How do you know?" Big Dog asked.

"I know," Paris said, smug in his knowledge.

"This river was discovered by Henry Hudson," Pee Wee said, showing off his knowledge of history.

"Wasn't," Paris disputed. "Indians were here already."

"He's talking about the first white man," Big Dog said.

"Wasn't Henry Hudson," Paris said. "First white man was an Italian guy named Verrazano. Henry Hudson explored it."

"Know so much," Big Dog said, annoyed. He hated not being the one who knew things.

"Know lots about this river," Paris said, proudly.

"Like—what else?"

"Like we fought the British along this river," Paris said. "See those . . . ?" He pointed to the old deserted shells of forts built just beneath the viaduct, along the Drive. "They were gun stations. We used to have our cannons pointed. *Boom, boom, boom*—blast them out of the water."

"Never heard of that," Pee Wee said.

"Never happened," Big Dog said.

"Sure it did. Know that traitor, Benedict Arnold?"

"Everybody know him," Pee Wee said.

"Well, he made good his escape to the British right here on this river."

"Right here on this very spot?" Big Dog said.

"Well—not right here," Paris said. "I think it had to be further up. This is a long river, you know."

"And you know just where he escaped?" Big Dog wanted to pin him down.

"Didn't say that."

"See?" Big Dog spread out his hands to Pee Wee.

"Look, this river is three hundred and six miles long. It goes all the way up—past the capital."

"New York is the capital," Big Dog said.

"Not true. Albany is. And even before you get there. The river's got canals and . . ."

"Paris, since you all moved to Riverside Drive, you think you know so much," Big Dog said.

For a moment Paris could only look at him. He looked just like Aunt Maud when he said that. Paris smiled. All the while he had thought Big Dog looked only like his father. "Well," Paris confessed, "Moms made me look all that up in the encyclopedia." He looked around, trying to remember the reason he had stood up, but the Day Line boat sailed by going up-river. "See that boat," he shouted, excited. "It goes all the way up to West Point."

"Oh, sweat," Pee Wee cried, getting excited too. "A fish." He was pointing at the old man who had caught a fish and was taking it, wiggling, from his line. "A big one."

"Only an eel," Big Dog said, disparagingly. "They no good—they just like snakes."

"They taste good," Pee Wee said. "One time my brother caught one, and my mother cooked it—hmmmmmm, good." He rubbed his stomach remembering.

"We don't eat eels," Big Dog said, shrugging his fat, smooth shoulders. "When my dad catches eels, he throws 'em back. We bring home only striped bass when we go fishing."

"You can catch striped bass here too," Pee Wee said. "My brother . . ."

"This water's polluted," Paris broke in. "You're not supposed to eat fish from here."

"We eat it," Pee Wee said. "Nothing happens to me."

"It's still polluted," Paris insisted. "Moms says they discharge all that nuclear stuff from the Indian Head plant down this river. If you eat the fish, you'll get sick."

"Look," Pee Wee made a muscle with a wiry arm. "Do I look sick?"

They looked at the arm. Big Dog said, "Pee Wee, why you so skinny?"

"Why you so fat?" Pee Wee hit back, poking a finger into the tight skin of Big Dog's arm.

Big Dog smirked at Pee Wee. He did look smaller, forlorn, even defenseless with his head bandaged.

" 'Cause," he said, "I don't eat polluted fish."

"And my mom said that now they got that sewage treatment plant right there," Paris pointed to the big domelike grayish structure a short distance down river, ". . . that the river is probably more polluted than ever." And as though in response the grinding machinery began its droning.

"Ugh." Big Dog squeezed his nose and moved his fat shoulders in his Aunt Maud way. "All that doo-doo and stuff? Who wants to live on Riverside Drive anyway?"

"My mother does," Paris said.

Chapter 5

They sat for a time in sympathetic silence, then Pee Wee pointed again. "He caught another one. Man . . ." Indeed, another fish was flashing from the fisherman's hook.

"Wish I could bring some home," Pee Wee said. "Bet my ma'd stay home and fix it for us. My ma loves fish."

"You'd bring home polluted fish?" Paris asked.

"Yep," Pee Wee nodded.

"If you want fish that bad," Big Dog said, "I'll catch some for you. I know how to fish."

"How you gonna catch 'em," Pee Wee asked. "With your hands?"

"No, make a fishing pole," Big Dog said. "My Dad taught me . . ."

"Oh, dad, dad, dad," Pee Wee sneered. "All that talk. Ain't never seen nothing he ever showed you."

"Bet if I had some string," Big Dog said. "I can find a pole."

"And bait, you need bait, you know?" Pee Wee said.

"You can dig for worms," Big Dog said.

"I still have my dollar," Paris offered impulsively. "What say I go up to Gus and buy some string?" Saying and thinking being the same, Paris jumped up and ran for the rail.

"What? You want to catch polluted fish?" Pee Wee reminded him.

Paris straddled the rail, thinking. "Did Frankie eat the fish your mother cooked too?"

"Sure he did. He brought 'em," Pee Wee said.

"He ain't little," Paris said, and jumping from the rail scooted around the strollers, running for the steps out of the park.

Racing up the hill to the avenue, Paris forgot all about the sun and its dip to the west. He no longer worried about work that had to be done. His mind was set on new adventure. He turned the corner, dashing into the little store that sold everything from groceries to hardware.

"Gus," he called to the big man behind the counter. "What kind of string do I need to make a fishing line?"

"Whatcha gonna catch?" The slow-moving man who never smiled looked down at him through half-closed eyes.

"Fish—eels and stuff."

"In that river?" Gus jerked his thumb west.

"Yeah," Paris said.

"Boy, you don't need no line for that," Gus said. "Just stand on the side of the river and the fish will float up—dead, ready for the pot."

Paris blinked, wondering if Gus really believed what

he was saying. "No," he said. "I seen a fisherman. He caught some—with a line."

"Then he ready to commit suicide," Gus said, blinking his half-closed eyes. Paris thought of protesting. He thought of telling Gus about Pee Wee—but more especially about Frankie. "We just doing it for the fun," he said instead.

"Best take care," Gus's voice rumbled over the counter. "Them fishes so polluted that just touch 'em and your hands liable to fall off." Unblinking, Paris kept his eyes on Gus, his mind on the fisherman with his lively wiggling fish. "But now . . ." Gus said. "If you insist . . ."

He waited. Paris kept staring at him, so Gus threw a roll of cord up to the counter. Paris handed him the dollar and waited.

"What you wants now, Mister-big-time-fisherman?" Gus asked.

"My change," Paris said.

"What change?" Gus narrowed his eyes. "Man, you owe me fifteen cents. Just figgered I'd let you—on account of it's the last time I might see you."

"One dollar for some string!" Paris cried. Big Gus raised an eyebrow, looking evil. "That's cheating," Paris said. "I'm never gonna come back to this old store again." He marched out of the store and around the corner.

"Thought that was you in Gus's, li'l punk." Paris jumped. He looked up. Marvin was standing before him,

his friends behind him. He looked around the crowded avenue. He was alone.

He thought of his mother. Of all that work he hadn't done. How could he have done it when he was out here being beaten up? Killed? But who was around who would know to tell her?

That thought made him desperate. He stared into Marvin's eyes, waiting for them to blink, to shift, so he could gain time to move. "What kind of loot you got for me, man?" Marvin asked.

"No—no—nothing."

"What! You got to be kidding," Marvin said, his mean eyes getting a meaner look. "You got to know you walk with something in your pocket when I'm around."

Money or not, he was in for it. Paris knew that Marvin would never forgive him for that episode with Frankie. Paris licked his dry lips. He tried to feel just where Russell was standing. Russell dared not stop him if he ran around him. Russell knew his mother. He'd be more scared of having folks know he had helped kill Paris than he was of Marvin. Still Paris dared not take his eyes from Marvin to look.

"Do we do him in here, Marve?" the strange boy said. "Or do we take him back to the shell?" Marvin's eyes shifted. And Paris scooted—back around the corner into Gus's store.

"Thought you'd be back, Mr. Fisherman," Gus greeted him. "Who ever heard of a fisherman fishing without hooks?" He pushed Paris some drapery hooks over the counter. But then he noticed Paris's fast breath-

ing, his wide-open-from-fright eyes. So he came from behind the counter and waddled to the door.

The boys had disappeared from the front of the
store. Gus stood outside and called, "I seen you, Marvin.
Ain't no use you hiding. I done tole you—don't you be
hanging—not two miles around this here store. Get my
hands on you, boy—turn you every way but loose. Hear
me?" He waited, listening, then waddled back in the
store.

"Them hooks'll be twenty-five cents," he said. Then
as Paris only stared, he said, "I'll trust you."

Paris went to the door and peered out. Was Marvin
waiting just around the corner? Or had he guessed where
they were playing and was waiting at the Drive? None of
the boys had walked past the store. . . .

"What you using for bait?" Gus asked.

"Worms."

"Ain't nothing wrong with that," he said. "If they
don't work, I got some good baloney. Fish goes for
baloney—some of 'em do."

Paris stepped out of the store. Gus called, "Yeah, be
careful of that worm, Marvin. I do declare that got to be
the evilest child in the world."

Imagining that he saw a movement at the corner,
Paris ran out of the store to the opposite corner. He
turned and heard, "Gotcha!"

Paris jumped—over the iron rail of the corner building and scooted into an alley. Standing between the first
two buildings of the street, he pressed himself against the
east building, scarcely breathing, waiting. Had they seen

him? Everything was happening so fast. Paris waited for them to pass. Seconds—a minute. He peeped out. And there was Angelo, the drunk, bending over laughing, his wide-open mouth showing the darkness of his toothless gums. Then Paris recognized Angelo's voice.

Still he couldn't chance the streets. Instead, he went to the back of the alley and scaled the wooden fence that separated the corner building from the rest of the buildings of the street. Lowering himself into the open courts that ran down to the Drive, he began to walk cautiously. Terror filled him at the snarling sounds of guard dogs in the basement apartments. Some bared their teeth at the windows as he passed. Others pushed noses through the iron gates of fences, trying to get out, to get at him. But the terror he felt was no match for the terror he had felt when facing Marvin.

Arriving at a building on the corner, he walked up some steps which at another time had been called the service entrance. Once again he peered out, searching the lonely pavements of the Drive. He measured the distance between where he stood and the parkside. Waiting for a break in the traffic, he bounded across the street and flew down the steps, thankful to hear the traffic close behind him.

He slowed down as he walked through the tunnel. By this time he was hot. New scratches stung his neck, and he was aware that the tear in his jeans had widened. But he was safe. For a while.

"What kept you so long?" Pee Wee said, when Paris joined him on the grass.

"Marvin," Paris said.

"Oh, man . . ." Pee Wee looked over Paris. "He didn't hurt you bad."

"He never touched me. I got this from climbing over the fence."

"Fence!" Pee Wee shook his head. He looked more like an orphan with his bandage dirtied from his digging in the dirt, and touching it with grubby hands. "We got to do something about that guy, Paris."

"Like what?" Paris asked.

"Stop him from making life miserable, that's what," Big Dog said.

"Like what?" Paris repeated, helpless.

"Get my brother after him," Pee Wee said. But they had done that, and now Marvin had more reason to get even.

"If I had been there," Big Dog said, "I'd have—*zip* . . ." he threw a punch. "Right in the back."

"And *voom,*" Pee Wee threw his. "I'd get him from the side."

"And *bop, tatatata,*" Paris had his turn. "To the chin, to the head . . ."

"Were his boys with him?" Big Dog asked. Paris nodded, his gloom returning.

"What he needs is for Frankie to get all the Dukes together one time—and take him apart."

"But your brother thinks that Marvin's too little," Paris said, feeling even worse. The boys in the Dukes were all between sixteen and twenty. They might scare

Then seeing how Big Dog was picking at the worms he said, "Hey, you don't even know how to bait a hook."

Big Dog's face was turned up in disgust, trying to touch the worms. Nevertheless, he kept trying. Then, as though his body reacted in fear, he turned to Paris. "Paris, can you put the worm on for me—please?"

"If you give us the bus fare to go to Central Park, I'll bait it for you," Pee Wee said.

"Central Park?" Big Dog cried. "To do what?"

"Catch crayfish," Pee Wee said.

"And leave me?"

"You can come with us," Pee Wee said. "You the one got the bus fare."

"But I don't want to go. I want to fish!"

"Can't, without bait," Pee Wee said, grinning.

Big Dog looked at Paris, accusing him. Paris shifted his eyes. He did feel guilty. But he didn't know if it was because of the trick Pee Wee was playing on Big Dog, or because he suddenly could see Pee Wee's tricks. Pee Wee had no right to trick Big Dog that way. They all had agreed to go fishing. They couldn't just run off and leave Big Dog, because he wouldn't give them bus fare. It wasn't right.

Paris studied Pee Wee's sad face beneath its dirty bandage. He looked from his face to his worn sneakers. Pee Wee never had any money. His mother never gave him any. Yet he almost always had his way. And it came to Paris that Pee Wee had had to learn how to have his way. Paris studied the flap of his torn jeans, then pulled it up to cover his bare knee.

"You don't have to help me," Big Dog said. "I'll do it myself." Big Dog pinched his little mouth, squinched up his face, picked up a worm, and with a look of spreading disgust, pierced its head with a loud squish. "I did it! I did it!" he shouted happily. Paris was happy too. Where did the kid get such a mind of his own? He was only nine.

"We can walk to Central Park," Pee Wee said, stubbornly. "It ain't that far."

But Paris was listening to his old friend with a new inner ear. He knew, suddenly, what his mother knew when she said Pee Wee led him astray. Pee Wee's next word would be bet. Paris had never been able to say no to a bet. So he said it first. "Bet I can beat you catching crayfish—right here in the river, Pee Wee."

"Ain't no crayfish in there," Pee Wee said, sulky that their roles had changed.

"How do we know? We ain't tried," Paris said. It wouldn't be easy to convince his friend. The thought of walking to Central Park had already opened up a whole new world in his head. Paris went to the guard rail and asked a passer-by for the use of his knife.

"What if there ain't," Pee Wee said. "And we waste all that time . . ."

"We can catch goopies," Paris said.

"Ain't no goopies," the disgruntled Pee Wee grumbled.

"Sure there is—goopies everywhere."

He liked that. He had learned to sidetrack Pee Wee when he hadn't even known he needed to sidetrack him before. After all, Pee Wee could go home whenever he wanted. No one cared.

Seeing Big Dog get up and move to the rocks, Paris called, "Careful, Big Dog. Those rocks are slippery."

"No, they ain't," Big Dog snapped. "It's not deep over there. Everybody knows you catch fish in deep water."

"What do we use to catch crayfish?" Pee Wee asked.

"In Central Park we use chewing gum," Paris said.

"We ain't got no gum," Pee Wee said.

Paris came back with two pieces of string and handed Pee Wee his. "Then we'll use worms," Paris said. "Goopies eat everything."

"No, they don't," Pee Wee pouted. "Their mouths too little." Nevertheless, Pee Wee cut a worm in half and handed Paris the other half.

They walked to the edge of the river and looked over as the fisherman caught another fish. "That ain't no eel," Pee Wee said.

"Maybe a striped bass?" Paris asked. "Is that like the one Frankie caught? Hey, Big Dog, look." He turned to where Big Dog had been standing a moment before. Only Big Dog wasn't there.

They looked back at the fisherman unhooking his flapping catch. Then they looked at the path behind them —then at each other.

Dropping their strings, they rushed to the rocks and jumping from one to the other, came to the front rock. "Gl—gl—gl . . . He—elp!" they heard from below.

Paris looked down and saw Big Dog bobbing around

on his stomach in the water. "You okay?" he called down.

Big Dog looked up, wide-eyed. His cheeks were pocked out with air, which he let out to shout, "He— elp," then he took another mouthful again.

Throwing themselves on the rock, the two boys reached down. Pee Wee's arm was too short. But although Paris's was longer, it didn't reach down far enough. "I'll hold your legs," Pee Wee said, going onto the other rock and throwing himself down so that he could wrap his arms around Paris's hips. Paris eased over. His hand touched Big Dog. He eased down further and grabbed his arm. But Big Dog's fat arm slipped. It was too big and too smooth to get a good hold.

"Tread water," Paris called. "Tread the water like I showed you last summer." Big Dog started treading the water. "Your hand," Paris called out. Big Dog reached up. At first Paris couldn't catch it. Then he did. He pulled. But instead of Big Dog coming up, Big Dog started pulling him over. He felt himself slipping through Pee Wee's little arms.

Paris snatched his hand from Big Dog's. Big Dog's eyes widened from fright. "Help me. Paris, help me . . ."

Paris braced himself, one hand against the rock. He waited for Pee Wee to get a tight grip around his legs. But he kept on thinking of Big Dog's weight and of the feel of Pee Wee's bony arms. He'd never make it. But neither could he let Big Dog drown—not alone. . . .

Big Dog looked tired as he kept up his dog paddle.

Paris reached down. Once again their hands moved around before touching. Then Big Dog grabbed hold. Paris pulled. Big Dog's weight seemed to pull Paris's arm from its shoulder. But now Big Dog's hold was desperate. He couldn't get free. Paris felt himself slipping over. Worse, Pee Wee, holding on to his legs, was going right along with him. . . .

Then suddenly Paris found himself sitting next to Pee Wee on the rock. He looked up and saw Big Dog in the air—fat and shining in the sun—a baby seal. Then he too was set on the rock beside them. The man with the floppy, canvas hat, his pipe in his mouth, stood looking down at them. They huddled together, staring back.

"Fishing's a right fine sport." The old fisherman grinned, his pipe caught between brown teeth. "But like all sports, can be dangerous. Got to remember," he nodded to Big Dog. "Never stand on a slippery rock. Even a goopie'll give you a fight if you snags it. They want to live too. . . ." He waited. Big Dog looked up, quiet. "Feeling all right now, young feller?"

"He's okay," Pee Wee answered. "He ain't swallowed no water."

"How you know?" Big Dog struggled out of fright ready to fight.

"Seen you holding your breath," Pee Wee said. "Anyhow, if you hadn't, that would have been stupid, stupid. Anybody knows you got to hold your breath if you fall in a river."

"At that you're lucky." The old man took the pipe out of his mouth and pointed it at Big Dog. "Boy, don't you ever forget, fat boys get drowned too. . . ." He walked off shaking his head, chuckling.

Looking at the sure-footed man walking over the rocks then making his way back to the tree, Paris wondered: was he just an ordinary old man or had he been there just to save their lives?

The old man sat back on his rock, his pipe in his mouth, staring serenely over his line into the water. Paris looked at Big Dog. Then he looked at Pee Wee. He looked back to the old man with his old, floppy hat. Then he looked up at the sun. "Got to go," he said. He got up, walked to the rail and climbed over. Looking back, he saw his skates. He climbed back and picking them up, put them over his shoulder. "Just got to go," he said.

Chapter 6

Paris walked fast. The heavy skates on his shoulder clanged. Every few steps he bent over to pull up the flap that refused to stay up. Now, his left knee had been rubbed thin on the rock as he was trying to save Big Dog. His knee was bruised. But what could he tell her?

His mother's eyebrows frowned down at him from over the cloud of her anger. Her mouth opened and shut, then refused to stay shut. He'd say he didn't know it was so late. And she'd say, "And-the-sun!" Jeeze! He'd rather she'd take the strap. When it came down, he'd scream. . . . After all she could be hitting him on top of another hurt. One given by a cop, or a kidnap . . .

A kidnapper? Paris's face brightened. That was it! He'd say he'd been kidnapped and had been taken far, far away—to some woods. He'd say that he had been tied up and that he had tricked his kidnapper. That's how he'd escaped. And he'd say he had run and run, then he got tired and had come to this old house in the woods and that he had knocked on the door and this old lady had given him food—and money to take a bus.

That was brilliant! More brilliant than anything Big

Dog could think up, betcha. Paris quickened his steps.
. . . And that's how his jeans got torn too. He'd hidden
in some brambles in the woods and when he had tried to
get out—they'd got caught . . .

Paris sighed, relieved. That took care of everything.
He'd even tell her that the brambles were near some
white birch trees. Moms had taught him how to tell white
birch. Happily, Paris saw the mouth, which had been
opening and shutting, opening and shutting, opening and
shutting, finally stay shut. She believed him.

Impatient now, Paris waited for the traffic on the
Drive to stop for him to cross. But as he went to the
other side he heard, "Paris—hey, Paris. Wait."

He stopped, but only for an instant. Recognizing Pee
Wee's voice, he walked on. He didn't want to talk to Pee
Wee. Everything that had happened had happened because of him. If Pee Wee hadn't come to the house, then
he wouldn't have gone out, then he wouldn't have seen
Big Dog, and nothing that had happened would have
happened.

Paris tightened his lips against his teeth. He walked
faster. But Pee Wee ran and caught up. "Man," Pee Wee
said. "What's gonna happen if we walk together?"

"It's late," Paris said. He didn't look at his sad-faced
friend, feeling that the little face might break his resolve
to go right home. "My mom will be . . ." he started to
explain. Then he tightened his mouth again. "It's late."

"Tole you not to worry," Pee Wee said. "I'm going
home with you to help . . ."

"No!" Paris stopped to stare at Pee Wee. His eyes wide, frightened. "You can't go with me!"

"Why?" The patch on Pee Wee's eyebrow shot up. The gauze had fallen off and now even the patch had blackened with dirt. "I promised . . ."

"Don't want you." Paris said, his face set, determined.

"What'd I do?" Pee Wee asked, his sad face bewildered.

"It's just too late," Paris said. "Moms's waiting . . ." Then he broke off. A witness! Of course! He needed at least one. "Could you come home and tell Moms that you saw me—and that I got kidnapped?"

"Kidnapped?"

"Yeah, tell her that you were going home . . . No, that you had just come from home and that . . ."

"Paris!" Paris turned. Joanne came walking toward them. "Where've you been all day?" she asked in a grown-up voice. "I just came from your house."

"My house?" Paris's heart skipped then beat faster. Forgetting that he really liked her and that he had always been shy before, he asked, "What were you doing at my house?"

"Your mother came to my house to ask if I had seen you. That was early. Said if you got home you could go to the reception with me. So I went to your house to see if you could. But she hadn't even seen you. Is she upset . . ."

Joanne was dressed for a party. In her pale blue dress with lace ruffled bottom, her shining patent leather shoes, topped by white fringed socks, he might even have thought her pretty—another time. But now the thought came that if he made Joanne believe, then he could make his mother believe.

"I been kidnapped," he said.

"Kidnapped?" Joanne looked all the way down at him from the height of her hastily stuck up head. "Who'd want to kidnap you?"

"Dunno," Paris shrugged. He stared straight into her eyes. "Some men," he said. "They held me—all day."

"What men?" Joanne asked. What a stupid question. He had always thought Joanne smart.

"How do I know," Paris said shrugging. "They were just walking by—and they grabbed me . . ."

"Walking!" Joanne's voice squeaked her disbelief. "Walking by where?"

"I mean driving," Paris corrected himself. "They took me, all the way . . ."

"Is that what happened to your head?" Joanne said, dismissing Paris and turning her attention instead to Pee Wee.

"My head?" Pee Wee asked, blinking. Then he put his hand on his patch. "Oh, my head."

"Yes," Joanne said. "Did they beat you on your head?"

"Who?" Pee Wee asked.

"The kidnappers," Joanne said.

"Kidnapper!" Pee Wee looked at Paris, his eyes stretched wide asking for clues. But what clues could he give with Joanne staring from one to the other, not believing him. Pee Wee was not the one who had been kid-napped. And why not? What was wrong with both of them being kidnapped? Paris stretched his eyes and gave Pee Wee a slight nod. And Pee Wee grabbed his head, ducking it to the side as though warding off other questions. "Yeah, yeah—kidnapper . . ."

"How long after I saw you did this happen?" Joanne asked.

"Right after . . ." Paris started then stopped as he heard Pee Wee saying:

"A good while after . . ."

"Did they kidnap Big Dog too?" Joanne kept asking questions as though she thought she was Sergeant Woodrow.

"Big Dog?" Pee Wee said, looking at Paris for more clues.

"Yes," Joanne said. "His mother was at our house looking for him. I told her I saw him with you two earlier."

"Oh, sweat," Paris almost groaned aloud. Aunt Maud too? "Yeah, Big Dog was with us. These guys came up, see? They jumped out of the car and snatched the three of us, see? They pushed us in the car and Pee Wee jumped out. They hit him over the head, see? Then I got out and ran. But they kept Big Dog . . . and . . ."

"Miss Maud said she went to see Pee Wee's mother," Joanne seemed to have stopped hearing what Paris was saying.

"She had?" Paris said. "What she say?" Even Pee Wee got interested enough to examine the tips of his sneakers, waiting for the answer. "That she hadn't been home all day," Joanne said.

"Anyway, I had to stay with Pee Wee in the hospital until they took care of his head."

"You okay now?" Joanne asked Pee Wee.

"Me? Sure I'm okay." He blinked.

"Then you weren't badly hurt?" Joanne asked.

"Oh, you mean my head? It feels—a li'l better," Pee Wee said.

"What you really need is a change of bandage," Joanne said sarcastically.

She turned to walk away, just as Big Dog came running across the drive shouting, "It ain't fair. It ain't fair. How you run off and leave me like that?"

He came waddling toward them, his pants soaking, shirt in hand. Clumps of grass and dirt clung to him and his water-logged shoes squinched with every wet footstep.

"What happened to you?" Joanne squealed.

"Almost drowned," Big Dog said proudly.

"The kidnappers tried to drown you?"

"Kidnappers?" Big Dog screwed up his face. "What kidnappers? Didn't these turkeys tell you what happened? I went fishing, see?" he said. "I couldn't catch fish on the grass, see? So I go on these big rocks, see? They were slippery. Then I went like this—" He drew his arm back, showing off how expert he was at casting his line.

"Paris and Pee Wee were with you?" Joanne asked.

"Sure. They tried to make like heroes trying to save me when I went in. They just weren't with it. Then here comes this old guy, see? He grabbed me—swoop—just like that."

Paris walked away from them dejected. Somehow he had been betrayed. Who'd believe him now? Joanne, Aunt Maud, Moms . . . And why?

"That Big Dog sure got a big mouth," Pee Wee said, as he caught up with Paris. "Tole you to leave him home."

"You told me! I told you!" Paris said, shouting. It hadn't been him; he knew that to take Big Dog out meant trouble.

Now his mother would say, "Paris you-are-not-responsible. How-could-you-let-that-happen to Big Dog?"

Was it his fault if Big Dog fell in the river? No. No more than it had been his fault when Pee Wee fell and hit his head. Or when . . . Then Paris recalled the screech of brakes in his ears, the hot air against his leg as the car stopped, the tugging of his jeans as they tore. He reached down to pull up the torn flap. *He had almost been hit by a car!*

Paris's face brightened. He could tell his mom that he *had* been hit by a car and that Pee Wee had come crashing down the hill and had hit his head. And that they had been taken to the hospital, and the doctors had kept them waiting—all day, on account of there being so many kids. And Big Dog? What about Big Dog? Well— all the while they had been in the hospital, he and Pee Wee had worried because Big Dog had been kidnapped, and they knew that the kidnappers had taken him down near the river.

Kidnappers? What kidnappers? That would be a lie!
. . . Anyway they knew Big Dog was down near the
river. And they were scared something bad might happen
to him. So they left the hospital and ran down to the river
—just in time to see him fall in—and they had tried to
save him. There—that was the truth—almost.

"Hey wait . . ."

"Here comes that big-mouth Big Dog," Pee Wee
grumbled.

But knowing that he would be believed again, Paris's
spirits soared. "Let's hide," he said.

They ran, ducking around the corner, and into the
side entrance of the corner building. Waiting, they flattened themselves against the wall, looking out to see
when Big Dog crossed the street.

They waited. Big Dog didn't pass. They waited. Big
Dog still didn't pass. Time passed. One minute. Two
minutes. Paris peeped out. No Big Dog. He pushed his
head out to look around the door. No Big Dog. Going
down the steps, he stood looking around. No Big Dog.
He walked toward the corner . . .

"Boo! Gotcha!" Big Dog sprang from where he had
been crouching behind the steps.

"Not fair. Not fair," Paris cried. "You cheat. Pee
Wee, didn't he cheat?" But Pee Wee hadn't followed. He
wasn't even standing on the steps. Big Dog and Paris
exchanged glances. They had ducked into the burned-out
building they called the shell. They never played in that
building. Without ever having been told, they knew play-

ing there was forbidden. So stepping back to look into the lobby of the forbidden place, Paris found that his heart was pounding.

But Pee Wee was right in the lobby. Kneeling, he was looking through the pile of blackened rubble heaped against the wall. "Look, Paris," he said, when he heard them walk up behind him. "Money! I found a quarter."

Big Dog and Paris knelt beside Pee Wee. They started to search the burned-out junk piled against the wall. Big Dog found a dime. Now the three started to search in earnest. Paris found a quarter.

"Oh, sweat," Pee Wee said. "Bet we can make our fortune going through this old house." He sat rubbing a coin clean on his jeans. A Kennedy fifty-cent piece.

"Oh, sweat," Paris said. "If we get enough money in here, I can tell my mom . . ." Then he shut up, deciding not to talk out loud around Big Dog. But the new thought kept growing: he could tell her he had gone out to find a job—for her. And he would have money to prove it!

But that pile of junk yielded nothing more. Only a pair of gloves burned through the fingers. Big Dog found a leather belt that had blackened but not burned. They were happy about these. But Pee Wee only wanted money. "Maybe we'll find more upstairs," he said. Without a word the three climbed the building to the second floor.

They tiptoed through large, empty apartments—larger than those in Paris's building. But most of the

rubble here had been swept away. So they climbed to the third floor.

Here the fire had burned through even the walls that had separated apartment from apartment. It gave a feeling of desolation to the floor, a waiting quality to the space. It had the feel of an empty playground waiting for kids to play; of a basketball court after the players had gone, leaving it thick with sweat, but so, so empty.

Ghosts. It had the feel of ghosts around them. Paris felt them. He felt them move from place to place. He sensed the ghosts waiting for them to restart their search, for treasure—*the* treasure. Paris wanted to see, to hear, to disrobe them, to tear off their sheets. But what if instead of old, evil landlords, they found skeletons?

On the fourth floor the apartments regained their separatedness. And as they went from room to room, their search for gold changed to an adventure. They came to a room with a lived-in look. "Jeeze," Big Dog shouted. "This got to be the room where Marvin and them big guys hang out!" Cigarette ends littered the floor. Whisky bottles stood beside bundles made into cushions, indented from sitting.

"Yeah," Pee Wee said, then went to the window. "Guess this must be where they be swinging from."

A rope outside the window hung from the roof to the side court of the building. "Oh, sweat," Paris said, looking down. "That's some swing."

"Told you that Marvin was crazy—or a stupid one," Big Dog said.

"Or brave," Paris said, remembering that Pee Wee was the one who had said brave. But the sight of the swinging rope gave a lilt to his heart.

"Don't have to be brave to swing from a rope," Pee Wee said, a look of caution springing to his eyes.

"Sure you do . . ." Paris knew now how to make Pee Wee make a dare ". . . real brave, or real strong one." Pee Wee shook his head. He kept shaking his head. And seeing Pee Wee wouldn't take the bait, Paris had to say, "Bet I can swing down to the court quicker than you."

Pee Wee's drooping face reminded Paris of a dog with its tail and ears flopping. But why should Pee Wee bet only when he thought he'd win? "Okay," Pee Wee said, giving in. "Bet."

"I'll go first," Paris said to show he was the bravest. It was true. The excitement of the dangling rope had forced him. He grabbed hold of it, wrapped one leg around, and pushed off with the other.

As he slid down his stomach rose to meet his chest —in pleasure. But half way, his hand burnt. He stopped. "You stopped. You stopped," Pee Wee called from the window.

So despite the pain of his hands, Paris let himself slide all the way to the court. He stood looking up as Pee Wee caught the rope. He slid down without stopping.

"Didn't it burn?" Paris asked.

"Uh-huh," Pee Wee said. They stood, comparing hands. The top skin had burned away from Paris's palm.

Beneath, the bottom skin showed a raw pink. On Pee Wee's tough hands, the skin had only been rubbed to a shine.

"Hey, what you guys doing down there?" Big Dog called down to them.

"Come on?" Pee Wee shouted back.

"Noooo," Big Dog said. "My ma don't have no stupid kid. Only a son that plays with 'em."

"Let's do it again," Pee Wee said, his excitement growing. Paris shook his head. "Bet I do it faster two times out of three," he said.

"Bet," Paris said, feeling droopy. But then he remembered the gloves in his back pocket.

They ran from the court, back around the corner, and into the burned-out shell of a building. They rushed up the stairs and into the room where Big Dog waited. Paris took the burned-fingered gloves he had salvaged and put them on. By that time Pee Wee was already at the window. "My turn first, Paris," he said.

Annoyed that his friend got to the window before him, Paris said impulsively, "Bet it's more fun from the roof."

"Now I know you crazy," Big Dog said. "Don't know why I hang around with you guys."

"Me neither," Pee Wee said, racing to catch up with Paris as he dashed from the room.

Getting out on the roof, Paris rushed to the wall over which the rope had been thrown. He climbed on top as Pee Wee came out. "That ain't fair," Pee Wee complained. "I'm the one supposed to be first, Paris. You went first the last time." Paris looked around at Big Dog. But Big Dog had just stepped out and was leaning on the door, tired. "Anyway," Pee Wee said. "I go first because I won."

Paris got down and stood looking down into the courtyard. From the roof of the seven-story building, the courtyard looked five times further away. A thrill of anticipation shivered through him. "Come on. Come on," he urged impatiently.

"I'm going. I'm going," Pee Wee said. But he took his time wrapping a piece of cloth he had picked up somewhere along the way, around his hands.

"Paris! Pee Wee!" Big Dog's voice higher than ever caused them to turn. "Look at this. Look at this!" Big Dog was holding on to the rope. Paris looked at where his fat friend was pointing and had an urgent need to pee. He searched for a spot. But was that what he really wanted? He twisted his legs together, staring.

The knot was secure. But the rope going around the pipe had almost completely unraveled from constant rubbing! All that was left were two strings holding it together!

Pee Wee and Paris kept staring, afraid to even touch it. Paris, his lips pulled up to his teeth, his eyes round; Pee Wee, the patch from his forehead down, almost to his eyes, giving the sadness of his face a look of defeat. Their eyes turned to Big Dog. Then without a word the three friends left the roof and walked, silently, down the stairs.

At the first floor, seeing his skates dropped during the search of rubble, Paris picked them up and followed

Pee Wee and Big Dog out of the building. They walked
an entire block down the Drive before any of them spoke.
Then Pee Wee ventured one word: "Ma–an . . ."

Paris saw no need to try better. What could he say?
The day was ending fast. A big ball of sun blazing in the
west had colored the water a bright pink. What to say?
Why had they stopped in that old burned-out shell of a

building? He had been on his way home, knowing Moms was already upset. What had made him stop?

Ghosts? He searched hopefully through the fragments of his mind for a plausible reason. What if I told her about the ghosts? They had made Pee Wee see that money. They had led him—and Pee Wee—astray. Or why else had they gone up those stairs of a building they had never dared enter before? Ghosts had saved their lives too. When they were ready to jump from the roof. *Jump from the roof!* "Don't-tell-me—that . . ." the mouth opened then shut.

Still, something had been around. Or what had stopped Big Dog from listening to Pee Wee and jumping out of that window—big as he was? And what if Paris had rushed from the rooftop, and had not listened to Pee Wee and tried to be fair? And what if Big Dog had decided they were too crazy—or stupid to be around and had gone on home. Then Pee Wee would have just gone on over . . .

Paris shook his head to rid his mind of the thought. His friend landing, one big splatter on the court below. He never wanted to be without Pee Wee. Pee Wee was his best friend in the whole world. What could happen worse to a boy than losing his best friend in the world? And as that question took importance in his mind, the thing worse that could happen, did . . .

Chapter 7

"See, you can't take Gus around in your pocket," Marvin's voice snarled. And they froze. Then they looked up at Marvin and from Marvin to his friends. Russell was still with him. But it was a different boy from the one earlier. He looked even tougher. "Li'l punk," Marvin sneered. "Why'd you get Gus after me?"

Paris struggled for his voice, but even when he had found it, it sounded tired. "Didn't," he whispered.

"Did. Sent him out to me. Thought he was big enough to do me in, didn't you?"

"Didn't," Paris repeated, fighting for a strong, tough note.

"Calling me a liar?" Marvin's voice got stronger as Paris's got weaker. He stepped to Paris. Instinctively, the three boys stepped back.

"I—I—went to the store to get—to get . . ." It was no use, his voice wasn't working anymore.

"You went into the store." Marvin said and smirked. "But you had to come out—sometime . . ." The evil smile on the boy's face shook Paris. He was thankful, though, that his eyes hadn't turned red. Still, he wanted to run. But where to? He looked at Russell, behind Marvin. Russell looked away, guilty. Marvin, reading his mind, leered. "Where you want to go—home? I'll give you a start."

And home was exactly where Paris wanted to be. He missed home. If he had it to do over again, he would never have left. He would clean and clean and clean . . .

"Lay off us, Marvin," Pee Wee said. But even Pee Wee's voice had lost its edge. It was as though the day had been drawn out too long. Too much had happened. They all were tired and needed the familiar feel of home. Paris would have gladly let Marvin beat him up—if he hadn't been so scared that the mean boy might stomp him to death, just for the fun of it.

"I ain't bothering you." Marvin spoke to Pee Wee. "I just want this li'l sucker, right here."

"If you touch him, I'll get my brother after you," Pee Wee said.

"Go on," Marvin challenged. "Go now. And while you getting him, make sure you tell him that I'll have a hamburger sandwich all ready when he gets here. Your snitcher friend here."

"Who's his brother?" the stranger boy asked.

"Frankie's the president of the Dukes, man," Russell said, a warning in his voice.

"Oh?" the stranger said, giving a sideways look at Marvin. "Don't want to be messing with them Dukes, man."

"What you scared of?" Marvin said. "You're with me."

"But if you mess with my friend, you messing with me," Pee Wee said, his courage fed by the respect shown at mention of the Dukes.

"Come on," Russell said, taking courage too. "These kids too little, man."

"He ain't too little," Marvin said, reaching out and grabbing Paris's arm.

"This morning? What were you saying this morning? Go on—make that fist again."

Paris remembered the morning. He remembered Pee Wee and Big Dog, planning their attack on Marvin. But did they remember?

"Marvin," Pee Wee said, obviously not remembering. "I got money. Got a quarter if you want."

"What's a quarter?" Marvin said.

"He's got a Kennedy fifty-cent piece too," Big Dog put in.

"Let's see," Marvin said.

"You gonna take my quarter?" Pee Wee said, glaring at Big Dog.

Marvin jerked Paris closer, shaking him. "Does he or doesn't he have a Kennedy?" he asked.

"I don't—" Marvin hit Paris across his mouth. Blood spurted and Paris could feel his lip swell. So here was the time he'd been waiting for with such dread. Marvin beating him up, maybe even killing him. If he hit back, it was sure—that would be the end.

"Lay offa him," Big Dog came at Marvin, shouting. "He ain't bothering you. Pee Wee, go get Frankie . . ."

"Okay, okay," Pee Wee said, reluctant to leave Paris. "Here's the old Kennedy piece, but just you wait . . ."

Instead of taking the piece, Marvin slapped Paris across his face again. "I can't fight you," Paris said. "You're too big."

"Too bad because . . ."

"The Dukes—man," the stranger boy said. "Marvin, you got to be crazy. Leave these kids, man . . ."

"Yeah," Russell spoke, following the stranger boy's lead. "Anyway, if we don't be getting to that ole building, we won't be able to do a thing. Sun's going down, man."

That made Marvin pause. He pulled Paris until their faces almost touched. "Boy, you in luck—this time. But watch out." He pushed Paris away, then snatched the skates from off his shoulder. "Next time, be carrying something valuable—know what I mean?"

The three boys stood at the corner, watching the bigger boys walk away, Marvin in the lead—bad, in control, sure of his toughness. They waited until they had gone the few short blocks, disappearing into the shell of the burned-out building, then they started on their way. For the first few seconds they walked in silence. Then Big Dog broke the silence to say, "I hate that guy, don't you, Paris?"

"Sure do," Pee Wee answered. "Hate his guts. Wait till I get home—gonna tell Frankie sure. Just wait."

"Think he's so bad," Big Dog said. "Wish something happens to him—something bad. Don't you Paris?"

But Paris was feeling too low to talk. He could feel the flapping of his torn jeans, and now the heaviness of his still swelling lips. All he could think about was his mother. He saw her mouth opening, shutting: "Everything I ever get you, you break up or throw away. Where do you think I get money . . ." Marvin had hit him. "Why did he have to take my skates?" he asked.

"Skates! Oh, sweat," Big Dog clapped his hand against his forehead. "Left mine down by the river."

"Jeeze, me too," Pee Wee said. "Got to get 'em." The two boys scooted off, leaving Paris alone. He looked after them as they crossed the drive, and kept looking as they became silhouettes against the blazing ball of the sun, before disappearing—as though swallowed up by the sun, down the steps leading to the river.

Paris trudged on toward home. He thought suddenly of the broken window he had left there. Had she seen it? The window, his jeans, and now his skates. What to say? She'd scold him. Punish him. She'd fuss and fuss and fuss . . .

Paris entered ¹   ding and rang for the elevator. He listened as it   , then began its descent—shaking, rattling. Paris felt a wetness rolling down to his chin, he wiped it, then looked at his stiffening, painful hand. Blood. God, he hated that guy. It seemed to him, then, that he had spent the whole day running away from Marvin, only to be caught at day's end by his worst enemy in the world.

And as Paris waited for the elevator, he wondered what to do to rid the neighborhood of the evil boy— forever. He could tell his mom again. Have her go to the police. They all had seen Marvin take his skates. He could even lie—adding something—like the little boy's bicycle. Say he had seen Marvin take it . . .

The elevator came rattling down to the ground floor, and like a fat man, settling into an uncomfortable chair, it rocked to a standstill. The door jerked half open, stopped, then slid back. Paris got in the elevator, pushed the button to his floor and waited. The elevator waited. After a long minute the door jerked half shut and stopped. Then started to slide closed.

But Paris's hand went out holding it back, holding it and holding it, until it slid all the way open again. Then he ran out of the elevator, and out of the building. He ran up the Drive, across the streets, sprinting over the blocks separating him from the burned-out shell of a building. Rushing into the lobby, he shouted, "Marvin, Marvin."

He heard the voices of the fourteen-year-old boys raised in laughter. He raced up the steps, hearing Marvin brag: "That's the way yo' got to treat li'l punks. Keep 'em shook up, so you don't have to kill 'em." And the mean laughter that followed.

"Marvin, Marvin." Paris ran up the first flight of steps, raced around the landing, then up to the second floor, still calling, "Mar–vin . . ."

"Sounds like somebody's calling," Russell's voice said.

Marvin laughed. "Them's ghosts, you hearing. That's all what hangs out in this creepy house. Ghosts— and fools like us . . ." Then the loud accompanying laughter.

On the third floor, Paris looked up the stairwell to shout, "Maar–vin. Maar–vin . . ."

"That *is* somebody calling." The voice of the strange boy spoke. And as Paris started up the stairs leading to the fourth floor, he looked up into the stranger's face. "What you want?" the boy asked, sounding uneasy.

"The rope," Paris gasped, slowing down, his breath coming hard. "It's dang'rous." He walked up the rest of the way, laboring as he went. But he made it into the apartment, then into the room where Marvin stood on the windowsill, rope in his hand, ready to step out on the ledge. "Don't, Marvin," Paris shouted, starting toward Marvin. But Russell grabbed him.

"What you want here, Paris? Man—go on home."

"Musta come for his skates," Marvin said.

"No!" Paris cried.

"Want me to give 'em to him?" Russell asked.

"You gotta be joking," Marvin said.

"His old lady'll beat his butt if he goes home without 'em," Russell said, knowingly.

"Tough!" Marvin's lips twisted into an evil grin. "But he in our territory now. She won't have to touch him when we get through with him." Marvin stepped to the ledge. But Paris broke away from Russell. He rushed to Marvin, grabbed him, pulled his other leg. "That rope —it ain't no good," he cried.

"Real anxious to get it over with, ain't you," Marvin said, trying to shake Paris's hand free. "But you just gotta wait till I gets back . . ." He fought for his leg. Paris held on. He fought again for his leg, then slid to the floor. "Should I waste him now? Or save him for dessert?" He spoke half joking, half angry. He didn't like the idea of his boys seeing him slip. But by that time the boys had heard Paris.

"Says the rope ain't no good, Marvin," the stranger boy said.

"What's he know?" Marvin asked.

"Don't hurt to check," Russell said.

"Okay," Marvin said, and he pushed Paris out of the room in front of him. "Let's get on, but if you messing with me, boy . . . You got to know that all things what go up—ain't got to come down—the same way."

Paris walked up the stairs with Marvin's words loud in his ears. What if the rope was whole again? What if he, Pee Wee, and Big Dog had seen it wrong? What if ghosts had made their eyes look at things the way they weren't. Marvin had said he'd throw him over. That's what he *had* said.

Would Russell let him? Help him? Would the stranger boy? Going up the remaining flight of steps, Paris kept feeling the combined strength of the boys at his back. How did he get down? No way—except over the roof.

Stepping out on the roof in the dwindling light of day, Paris looked over the blood-red river to New Jersey. How beautiful. A lovely view. His mother's view. His mother loved her view. He did too. He liked the way the New Jersey buildings, with the warm spring sun behind, looked dark, mysterious. And Moms had said that from New Jersey, the windows of Manhattan would be sparkling pink. Paris felt an instant sadness, the loss of something precious, not to be watching the sunset with his mom.

He led the boys to the tarpaulin-wrapped pipe, around which the rope was tied. Paris stood watching.

Russell stepped up and examined it. He turned the rope this and that way, looked at the knot. Jeeze! No one had to look that long to see that rope was frayed. The strange boy took the rope next, examined it—the knot. He too kept looking. Paris grew tense, ready, as Marvin stepped from behind him to stand with his friends. Paris waited much in the way that he and his friends had stood earlier —until the three were lost in thought. Then he bolted.

Bounding back into the building, Paris raced down the steps, taking two at a time. He was already at the second floor when he heard, "Catch him. Catch him." Footsteps thundered after him, some taking entire flights at a time.

But now Paris, his feet moved by fear, flew light as air down to the ground floor and out into the streets. In his desperation not to lead them home, he ran up one street and down another, up one street, down another. He alone in the world. He against all those others.

And suddenly he no longer feared them. Indeed, he no longer heard hard pounding feet chasing him. Then along with his fear, his strength also fled. Like a car running out of fuel, he stopped and slumped against a doorway too tired to think.

In little gasps he pulled fuel back into him. Little by little he revived, gained strength. Then little by little he began to think again.

Trudging home, he flipped through all the stories he had been thinking of during the day. Which one to use? They had all seemed so good at the time. But now all were like fragments, chasing around his mind to make a complete whole.

But Paris knew the right one had to come. When he stood in front of her, his mind would open and one would pop into his mouth. The one she wanted most to hear. He'd know because when her mouth finally shut to stay —then her ears would open up . . .

By the time Paris arrived at his building, the sun had slipped out of sight behind the New Jersey buildings. Only long, pink rays coloring the clouds held onto a bit of the day. Soon they, too, would vanish—then complete darkness.

Walking across the lobby, Paris pushed the button and listened as the sigh signaled the elevator's descent. He leaned against the cage, praying that it came before the final dark. But that instant always came so quickly.

"Hey, kid . . ." Paris spun around. The three big boys were stepping on three sides of him, his back was to the elevator cage.

The day had been too hard. Paris was tired. All he wanted was to surrender. Get it over with. Marvin stepped up to him. Paris looked into his enemy's face, showing him, by his expression, he could do what he wanted. He, Paris, had had it.

"Here," Marvin pushed out his hand. Automatically, Paris reached out and took his skates. "You sure a hard guy to catch up with," Marvin said. And nodding, he walked out. Marvin's friends nodded, too, but with a smile—a sort of thank you. They followed Marvin out.

Paris looked at the door closing behind them. He

kept looking, expecting them to push back in. The elevator creaked to a stop.

The door of his apartment opened as Paris was trying to fit his key in the lock. And there she stood. He had been seeing her like that all day long; standing, tall, blocking his way into the house, hands on hips, eyes blazing.

Paris eased himself into the apartment under her burning gaze. Then he stood, his back against the wall holding on to his hands for support.

"Start talking," she said, her mouth snapping open and snapping shut. "You-are-not-getting-away-with-it-this-time," she said. "Oh-no-you're-not! Do you know how long I've been home? Do you know how worried I've been? Do you see what time it is? I've been out of my mind! I go out to work every day to make things nice for you—for us. And all you think of doing is to go hanging out in the streets! Where were you? Okay, Paris, start talking and-you-better-make-it-good-this-time."

"I—I—I . . ." Paris swallowed. Tears welled up in his eyes. "I—I—I," he searched his mind. But words had wiped themselves off—completely. Big tears rolled down his cheeks. His body shook and then the sobs. He gave in to crying, crying, crying . . .

"Paris—baby, what happened?" she asked. She fell to her knees. "What happened out there on those mean streets to my baby?" She pulled him to her. Held him. He felt her soft bosom against him. He pressed his cheek against her. His arms went around her neck. He held on, never wanting to let go of the good feel of her, her softness, the good mother smell of her. "Come, come, tell Moms what happened to her most precious boy . . . ?"

"Moms, oh, Moms," Paris sobbed. "Why do you always have to go to work? I miss you . . ."